To Omm[illegible] –

Dymuniadau Gorau

oddiwrth,

Rewyn.

Do Come In!

A light-hearted look at parish life

Evelyn Evans

AuthorHouse™ UK Ltd.
500 Avebury Boulevard
Central Milton Keynes, MK9 2BE
www.authorhouse.co.uk
Phone: 08001974150

All characters are fictional .... But, should you detect a certain resemblance to yourself, a family member or a friend, then congratulations......for, such as these are among the number of Church-goers in the Province of Wales.

First published by AuthorHouse 1/29/2011

ISBN: 978-1-4520-4857-4 (sc)

This book is printed on acid-free paper.

Dedicated to my mother, Eva Ann Hughes, whose love of literature spanned almost a century, and whose faith and belief have inspired my own Christian journey.

Foreword

This is a light-hearted look at life in a parish from the viewpoint of the Vicar's wife. In a series of vignettes, Evelyn Evans manages to draw the reader into the fictional Parish of St Mary Magdalene in the small country town of Rhydbrychan in South Wales. Here she describes the vicar, his wife and some of the parishioners. Many of them are all too recognisable!

However underlying the sense of fun characterised in the writing there is also a serious message and a sense of spirituality. The chapters describing the parish pilgrimage to the Shrine of Walsingham, and the conversion of the new neighbours next door to the Vicarage, speak of the way people are nurtured and encouraged into a life of faith. That is outreach and evangelism at its best. The need for change and hope are portrayed through humour which is a necessary quality any parish priest needs to possess.

The author manages to convey the cohesion, sense of solidarity and the refusal to take themselves too seriously that are present in most South Walian parishes. And the book shows how it is through ordinary everyday relationships and encounters that God can be found.

+Barry Cambrensis
Archbishop of Wales.

Acnowledgements

First and foremost, I would like to thank my editor, Dr Fiona Parsons, who has made the admirable transition from marking and correcting narrative written by those studying the work of reputable theologians to editing an imaginary text, written by someone who has been immersed in raffle tickets, strawberry teas and harvest suppers for the best part of forty years.

Thanks are also due to Jane Smart, a friend and former teaching colleague, for the art work which illustrates each chapter.

Thanks, also, to my daughters, Rebecca and Claire for their listening ears over the telephone. Any omissions they may have suggested have definitely been included!

Thanks are also due to Mr. John Hobbs (a real life parishioner) for his assistance with technicalities.

Last, but by no means least, I would like to thank Mrs Angela Bolton MBE and Mrs Christine Ross, two wonderful friends who have given me so much encouragement during my time of writing. Just like the disciple Thomas, though in completely incomparable circumstances of course, they saw and they believed.

Contents

PART 1: 2001 **1**

Chapter 1: OMEGA and ALPHA **2**

Chapter 2: NO PEACE FOR THE WICKED? **34**

Chapter 3: THE MOTHERS' UNION CHRISTMAS CONCERT. **58**

PART 2: 2002 **87**

Chapter 4: WORKMEN AND SCAFFOLDING **88**

Chapter 5: MID-SUMMER LUNCHES **115**

PART 3: 2004→ **157**

Chapter 6: THE PARISH PILGRIMAGE **158**

Chapter 7: NEW NEIGHBOURS **202**

Parish Profile

The imaginary Parish of St Mary Magdalene is located in the small country town of Rhydbrychan in South Wales. It is about seven miles from the market town of Trehyfryd and approximately fifty-five miles from the cathedral city of St Deiniol's. It appears to have a very vibrant community and all new residents to the town are warmly welcomed, Welsh or English speakers alike.

'We are just like one big family here in Rhydbrychan,' said Mari Morgan, before she emigrated to Australia earlier this year. (Cambrian Evening News, May 22nd)

Clergy Revd Bryn Jenkins MA,M.Phil. (Vicar)
Revd Jeffrey Morgan (NSM priest)

Churchwardens Dr Huw Martin (Vicar's Warden)
Mr Meirion Lloyd (People's Warden)

Reader Mr Thomas Matthews

Licensed to administer the Chalice Mrs Beryl Francis

Organist Mrs Pat Lewis

Sunday School Superintendent Mr James Elliott

Parochial Church Council

Chairperson	Revd Bryn Jenkins
Secretary	Mr Meirion Lloyd
Treasurer	Mr Thomas Matthews

Members

Mrs Beryl Francis	Miss Lucy Richards
Mrs Lillian Shanks	Mrs Pat Lewis
Mr Ken Thomas	Mrs Martha Jones
Mr Charles Harris	Mrs Hilda Grey
Dr Huw Martin	Mrs Ida Phillips
Mr Phil Pugh	Mrs Chris Pugh

Revd. Jeffrey Morgan (ex-officio)

Organisations

Mothers' Union 1st Monday of each month at 7.00 pm in the Parish Hall **Branch Leader** Mrs Beryl Francis, telephone number 007002
Men's Society 2nd Tuesday of each month at 8.00 pm in the Parish Hall **Chairman** Revd Jeffrey Morgan, telephone number 007592
Sunday School Every Sunday at 9.30 am **Superintendent** Mr James Elliott, telephone number 007654
Flower Guild 3rd Monday of each month at 7.30 pm in the Parish Hall **Chairperson** Mrs May Roberts, telephone number 007543

Requests for Baptisms, Wedding Interviews and Confessions are by appointment with the Vicar. Please contact the Vicar directly on 007007.

PART 1
2001

DO COME IN!

CHAPTER 1:

OMEGA AND ALPHA

HAPPY RETIREMENT
GOOD LUCK

Rejoice in the Lord always, and again I say rejoice.

Let us give thanks to the Lord our God for it is meet and right so to do.

Such were the thoughts of Jennie Jenkins as she sat at her desk for the last time of her teaching career. Or maybe even

Whoop it up

Paint the town red

Let your hair down

Make merry

Having had a long innings in the school she felt truly blessed and silently offered to God a prayer of gratitude for a career that she had found both fulfilling and rewarding. Shortly she would leave her classroom to play the piano for her final assembly at Ysgol Brynglas. After twenty five years of teaching music and drama at the school she was now about to abandon ship. Age had caught up with her and within the hour she would be a retired teacher. She surreptitiously glanced at her watch. Shortly she would bid a fond farewell to the piano and the piano stool that had provided her bread and butter for over a quarter of a century. She could hardly believe how quickly the years had flown by. It seemed that it had been but in the twinkling of an eye that the years had passed by and now there were only minutes, as opposed to years, of service left to complete.

'Would you switch off the DVD please Christopher?' she asked. 'We'll soon be going down to the hall, and we need to put the television in the cupboard for the holiday and make sure that we leave the classroom nice and tidy.'

Her class had been watching a Disney sing-along film. She had given them a choice between the sing-along DVD and Benjamin Britten's "Young Person's Guide to the Orchestra"; the latter had lost by 9 -1 but Christopher had taken the defeat remarkably well, despite the fact that he had stated how much he liked to see the trombones.

'That's the brass section isn't it Mrs. Jenkins?' he had asked. 'Excellent, Christopher! Well done! You're quite right.'

Although he had been willing to go along with the majority vote Jennie knew that he would now be only too pleased to switch off Mickey Mouse and Friends.

'Leave it on!' screamed Ioan. 'We haven't got to my favourite bit yet.'

'Please Ioan, not now,' said Jennie brusquely. 'We need to stack the chairs and put everything away. Would somebody pick up that pencil please? - and look - there's a piece of paper down there. Please would you all do something to help?'

'Shall I check the drum-kit Miss?' asked Jonathan.

'No thank you Jonathan. You checked it straight after lunch, remember? But you can close the stage curtains if you will; that would be really helpful.'

She walked over to where the comfortable chairs were arranged - those designed for 'time out' or group sessions - and sat down thoughtfully. She knew that she was going to miss all the pupils, along with their behavioural difficulties, particularly this small class that had been her pastoral group for the past two years. 'Right everybody, when you've finished tidying up you can come and sit over here with me.'

Christopher was the first to get there and he chose the seat to Jennie's left. Amy and Rhys ran for the chair on her right with Rhys winning by a hair's breadth. Daniel, Ioan and Emma came to sit down, followed by Jamie.

'Mrs. Jenkins,' sang Emma, 'Can you change your mind? I don't want you to go. I'm not singing in the choir for no-one else.'

'It's time for me to finish now Emma,' replied Jennie soothingly. 'I have been here a very long time. As you know, your mother was a member of my choir many years ago, so that goes to show how old I must be.'

Emma was almost at the point of tears. 'But it won't be the same without you. Please come back after the holidays.' She paused for a moment. 'My Nan's much older than you and she's still working. She told me she works down the Bingo. She goes down the Bingo to work every night. She gave me a tenner once when she had a bonus.'

Jennie had her own thoughts about Nan's supposed employment and the bonus received. 'You will all be in my thoughts for a very long time to come,' replied Jennie. 'This class has made my last year of teaching a very happy one. Thank you.' She paused a moment to reflect. 'In fact it has been one of my happiest years ever, and last year too of course. We've all been together for quite a long time haven't we? Anyway you'll still have Mrs. Griffiths with you.'

Mrs. Ann Griffiths had been working alongside Jennie as the learning support assistant for the class and together they had made an excellent team; they had complemented and supported each other throughout this period and had enjoyed a great deal of fun and camaraderie.

'It won't be the same never again,' mumbled Emma.

'I like Mrs. Griffiths anyway,' said Amy. 'She's kind.'

'Why didn't she not never come to school today then?' asked Jamie.

'She's gone to a *fun-der-al* up England.' answered Daniel.

'Quite right, Daniel. Mrs. Griffiths has had to go to a funeral today.'

'Mrs. Griffiths is OK, but I prefer you,' said Rhys with a big grin. 'My mother said you got the patience of Joe, but she never told me who Joe was. I think it might be Jesus's dad.'

Jennie didn't want to embark on a theological discussion right at the end of the academic year, so a brief silence followed. 'Lewis! Jonathan!' she called, 'Please would you join us over here. We'll soon have to make our way to the hall and we all want to be ready don't we? We don't want to keep anybody waiting do we?....especially when we're finishing a little bit earlier than usual.'

Reluctantly, and at a snail's pace, Lewis joined the group. Jonathan meanwhile had taken up residence in Jennie's chair and was mouthing something to Rhys. By the look on his face Jennie was convinced that whatever was being suggested was far from complimentary.

'I don't want you to go neither,' said Lewis. 'You're the only teacher I've ever had who hasn't shouted at me for saying that swear word. You always say, 'now, that's not nice is it?' And you say it in your normal voice. Mrs. Gibbs screamed at me in the dining room just now and it only slipped out when I was eating my afters.' Lewis had been the most challenging pupil of her long career, but he had won her heart when he joined the class two years before. She was calling the register and had encountered what she believed to be a clerical error. The conversation that had followed had been somewhat confusing.

'Lewis!'

'Yes Miss?'

She had looked at Lewis and had taken another look at the register. 'Now listen, everybody, I want to be sure that I have your correct name on the register, so Lewis, please can you tell me your Christian name and your surname, that's your first name and your last name.'

'Lewis Lewis,' he replied, twitching his nose and wringing his hands. He appeared rather nervous and ill at ease; consequently Jennie thought that perhaps she wasn't making herself clear. She wondered if the boy had some sort of impediment or lack of self esteem, which is only to be expected in a special school. She breathed deeply before making a final attempt. 'I'm sorry to have to keep on like this my love. but…..'

'I'm Lewis Lewis,' he had bellowed in response. 'My father is Lewis Lewis, my grandfather is Lewis Lewis and my great grandfather was Lewis Lewis. Have you got a problem with that?' Jennie had been just about to offer some reassurance when Lewis continued. 'And my father told me that when I have a kid I got to call him Lewis Lewis to keep the family name. I told him point blank, I'm not getting married, I hate girls, so that's the end of it. There won't be no more Lewis Lewis never!'

Jennie smiled at her young pupil. 'Come here a moment Lewis Lewis.' As he began to walk towards her desk she had immediately repeated 'Lewis Lewis.'

'You got it wrong!' he had said impatiently. 'It's not Lewis Lewis Lewis Lewis! It's just Lewis Lewis. Lewis twice, not four times like you said just now.'

'Thank you Lewis,' Jennie had said. 'I must have been repeating myself.'

Nonetheless, it was the beginning of a good relationship.

Just as Jonathan was about to join the group the buzzer sounded, summoning everyone to the hall. Jennie noticed that he had an evil expression on his face and he seemed to be dragging his feet with intent.

'Thank you for closing those curtains *so nicely* Jonathan,' she said. 'My word, you've done a tremendous job there. Thank you very much indeed.'

Suddenly Jonathan caught hold of her hand and asked politely, 'Please can I carry your music?'

'Thank you very much Jonathan. That's most kind of you,' Jennie replied.

Disagreements and squabbles were short-lived when Jennie was around; because of her placid and composed nature she radiated an air of tranquillity in even the most difficult of circumstances. She very seldom felt the need to raise her voice but communicated in her customary manner, therefore situations generally remained controlled. She also had a very good sense of humour, which proved to be a valuable asset, not only in her work as teacher but also in her role as vicar's wife. She often attempted to lighten Bryn's load with an anecdote or a funny story.

'You are so witty, Jen', Bryn had said on numerous occasions.

Her colleagues, too, had appreciated her conviviality and had expressed how much her raucous laughter would be missed in the staff room, not to mention some of the jokes she had shared.

As Jennie walked with her class down the corridor she could tell that there was pandemonium coming from the school hall. She assumed that most of the teachers could not have accompanied their classes to assembly though it was quite clearly part of their job description. Jennie supposed that the majority of them were doing a quick change in their classroom cupboards ready for a speedy getaway to their end of term binge; twenty five years ago she had been doing the very same thing. When she got to the hall she could see the headmaster, Mr. Gerald Thompson, standing on the stage grinning like a Cheshire cat and asking everybody to be quiet. The problem was that there was so much noise nobody could hear what he was saying.

Jennie, with only minutes of her career left, decided not to intervene. Her farewell assembly the day before had been so different. Everybody had been well behaved and had listened attentively to the many speeches that had been made. She had been showered with gifts and cards and flowers and had been presented with a special book containing twenty five years of memorabilia. She had been given a send off that was second to none and she had barely concealed her emotions when Lewis Lewis made a presentation of luxury bedding and gave her a fond kiss on the cheek.

'You don't have to come back here no more. You can stop in bed and think of me…of us I mean,' he had said gruffly. Now however, amidst the uproar, Jennie hurried to the piano and began to play a voluntary. Slowly things began to calm down, but not before someone threw a heavy bag from somewhere in the auditorium. It landed on the stage with a wallop, missing the headmaster, Mr. Thompson, by no more than an inch.

'Who threw that?' he asked plaintively, but there was no response. The bag happened to belong to fragile little Luke Brown, and there was no way that he could have found the strength to throw it himself. He had brought some games to school that day and that was the reason for the bag being so much heavier than usual. It must have been thrown by Dan Marsh, a very badly behaved year 10 pupil, who had deliberately broken a window in the science room only days before. He was notorious for his appalling manners and extremely bad behaviour, and most members of staff dreaded seeing him come through their classroom door.

As Jennie glanced up from her music she could see him standing on a chair at the back of the hall; he was making obscene gestures and laughing. Unfortunately the whole of the back row was responding to his stupidity. He cupped his hands around his mouth and began to chant 'Gerry-o! Gerry-o!' Fortunately, at that point, several teachers came into the hall, including Mr. John Williams who was head of the P. E. Department, and to whom almost every pupil showed a high regard and admiration. Dan Mash immediately stopped his nonsense and sat down.

A sudden silence fell as the pupils listened respectfully to Jennie's final performance. As she was drawing Handel's Largo to an end there was a loud wolf whistle from the back of the hall, possibly provided by Dan Marsh, although no investigation was made. Jennie raised her eyes from the music score to see Miss Ellen Wilkins come teetering down the centre aisle towards the row of chairs in which her pastoral class was seated. She was clad in the skimpiest leather skirt and the highest high heeled shoes that Jennie had ever seen. Fortunately for Miss Wilkins, the group of children sitting in front of her provided a sort of safety curtain between herself and the eyes of the headmaster; otherwise she may well have ruined her chances of promotion!

The assembly was short. Following a rousing rendering of 'He's Got the Whole World in His Hands' the head-master offered a short prayer asking for God's blessing on all those gathered, with an additional request that the same may be ready to help and lend a hand wherever it was needed during the summer break. To bring the short Act of Worship to a close Jennie was asked to say 'The Grace' and then the pupils were escorted to their respective taxis to begin the summer vacation.

It was with mixed feelings that Jennie returned to her empty classroom to collect her belongings, along with the cards and the floral arrangements that she had been given earlier in the day. She stood still and appreciated the silence, and took in the ambience of what had been her home away from home for so long. Had it not been for the pending General Inspection, she may well have continued working there for a few more years. However, she didn't feel like updating schemes of work and school policies, attending an increased number of staff meetings and working parties and then going through all the strain and stress that accompanies such an evaluation. If she hadn't managed to raise standards or enable pupils to reach their full potential during her years of service at Ysgol Brynglas, then she had no right to call herself an educator. Jennie did not want to be placed in the hands of inspectors who would be gate crashing on her lessons, and to have to listen to their jargon for a complete school week was above and beyond the call of duty. Life was too short for that. She thought it best to take early retirement and begin to focus her energies on the unpaid employment that would be available to her 'on tap' 24/7 and 335/12! Such were the expected working hours of those engaged in the priesthood and her husband Bryn was no exception. She took a deep breath and walked out through the doors of her music and drama studio for the last time.

When Jennie reached the car park she could see that it was almost empty. Most employees had left the premises faster than the speed of light; they wanted to make the most of the six week break. As for Jennie, she lingered just a little; she wanted to make the most of these final moments. She had, as it were, reached the point of no return.

The journey from Ysgol Brynglas to Rhydbrychan took almost an hour, so it was about 4 o' clock when Jennie turned the key in the lock of St. Mary Magdalene Vicarage. She went straight into the kitchen, placed her cards and the floral arrangements on the worktop and switched on the kettle. There was no need to prepare an evening meal because Bryn had suggested that they ate at 'Yr Hen Efail' as a sort of celebration dinner. Only that morning, when Jennie was about to leave for her last day at school, Bryn had stressed the importance of acknowledging her dedicated service to the school and the day that she retired. She had gone out through the front door that morning as a working woman and had just returned through it pensioned off. Such was the way of the world; time would stand still for no-one. One had to make the most of every minute of every day. Jennie checked that all her floral arrangements had plenty of water then she lay on the floor with the intention of doing some relaxation exercises. She had observed a former colleague demonstrating warm-up activities prior to a P.E. display in the sports hall, and thought that now was a good a time as any to have a go. She could hardly believe that she was 'thinking school' so soon after retiring, but she felt that it was important to unwind before Bryn came home from his meeting. For Jennie, the week of parties, celebrations and farewells had left her feeling rather tense, even a tad downhearted if she were to be completely honest. She tried to remember some of the exercises that had been demonstrated.

She immediately called to mind the backward bend that Menna had performed so gracefully, but decided that it was far beyond her capabilities. She lay on her back and remembered the leg exercises, first up gently with the right leg, then down, next up gently with the left leg, then gently down. Then it was both together, followed by the cycling experience, moving slowly to begin with but becoming faster and faster, as if participating in some sort of cycling event. She repeated this exercise several times, during which her thoughts were filled with the choices of starters, main courses and deserts that were served at 'Yr Hen Efail'.

Jennie had decided on her order - it was to be home-made soup of the day, duck in orange sauce with a selection of vegetables, chocolate pavlova and cheese and biscuits to finish. As she began her fifth attempt at this exercise she thought that she heard a knock on the window pane, but decided that it must be a figment of her imagination, or even her hip bones creaking due to lack of regular work out, so she decided to proceed. She was delighted with the way the cycling experience was going; the speed was phenomenal considering that she was a mere novice. The next step was to lie very still and become aware of one's own breathing and nothing else. She repeated the exercise and it was when she was lying still that she heard a voice calling 'Yoo-hoo!' - followed by an equally melodic – 'Hello-o!' that she realised that she had company. There was 'someone out there' trying to attract her attention, but she was reluctant to bring this means of relaxation to such an abrupt end.

Even so Jennie got up as quickly as she could and looked towards the kitchen window. She had been observed by none other than the Right Reverend Anselm Thomas, Bishop of the diocese of St. Deiniol's. He clapped his hands enthusiastically and gave her a beaming smile. Jennie felt quite embarrassed. As she went to unlock the back door she wondered what on earth had possessed her to be so impetuous as to execute such reckless behaviour in the vicarage kitchen!

'*Do come in* Father,' she said. Jennie just couldn't bring herself to use his name; this wasn't so much out of respect but out of awkwardness. How loving parents could inflict such a name on their child was unbelievable. Apparently they had chosen the name David but, because three of the babies sharing the four bed maternity ward in Ysbyty-y-Bro were given that same name, his mother had decided to go for something completely different, just in case there was any mix up with the newborns! 'Anyway,' she had assured him in his early years, 'there was a thirteenth century bishop named Anselm. Everybody knows that!' Nevertheless, the name often managed to raise eyebrows….and laughs! Chris Pugh had said, at every Confirmation Service, that he was 'andsome by name and 'andsome by nature, and he was known by some of the clergy as 'andsome Tom. Unfortunately, his parents had not given him a middle name to fall back on. At least he knew that, unlike other poor mortals, he would continue to be 'andsome until he took his last breath!

'Would you like a cup of tea or coffee Father?' asked Jennie. 'Bryn shouldn't be long, especially if he's expecting you.'

'As a matter of fact he's not expecting me at all,' he replied. 'I had a lift down with Martin the Dean. We've got that all important meeting in Pont Gwallter tonight, so he's made a short detour to visit his daughter Sian-Eirlys on the way. I thought I'd have a lift from here with Bryn if that's alright.' He paused. 'One of these days I'm going to get my L plates.'

Jennie barely heard this remark; she was trying to come to terms with the fact that the celebration dinner was off and that Bryn would be escorting the bishop to an all important meeting. She was not amused.

'Did you say tea or coffee?' she asked.

'I didn't,' was the reply. 'If it's all the same with you I'll have the usual...and a cheese sandwich if there's one going. I'm *starving*!' She was surprised that a man in his position could use the word so flippantly. Jennie poured him a very large whisky - as was his usual - and proceeded to make him a wad of cheese sandwiches and cut three generous slices of chocolate sponge. It was known throughout the diocese that Bishop Anselm had a very hearty appetite and would probably eat a horse if he was offered one! He always happened to have an empty carrier bag in his suitcase along with his mitre, cope and collapsible crozier, and this proved to be invaluable when parishioners had over-catered for the receptions following the many services at which he presided. In some parishes fruit cakes were set aside for him to take home with him to the palace; they didn't even make it to the tables!

At Christmas time his living room looked very much like a saloon bar with the variety of bottles of spirits and beers that he had been given to mark the festive season. He had always maintained that there had only ever been two women of note in his life, his mother and the Virgin Mary, and he always raised a glass to their memory as soon as he returned from Mid-night Mass. As he was now approaching his mid-fifties it was highly unlikely that a Lady Godiva or even a Farmers' Market Dairy Queen would cross his path!

Jennie poured herself a glass of red wine and sat opposite him. She enjoyed his company, particularly when he expressed how hard working a cleric was Bryn and how he must spend most of his waking hours engaged in his priestly duties. Today was no exception. 'If every vicar in the diocese worked as hard as Bryn then we'd be the most thriving part of the Province.' In view of such comments and observations Jennie couldn't comprehend how he had not yet been made a Canon of the Cathedral. She had half expected to hear that, after the death of Canon Llewellyn Price, Bryn would be given the seat of Cadwalader, but it was not to be. Instead it was offered to Dai Trent, who had been installed during an impressive Choral Evensong some months before. Jennie decided to take the opportunity to inform the bishop of Bryn's ceaseless endeavours to obtain a lottery grant so that the necessary structural work at St. Mary Magdalene`s could begin. He had also been in touch with a number of charities, but Jennie didn't know if there had been any response as yet. She went on to eulogise generally about how the parish was moving forward under Bryn's strong leadership. She added that the Alpha Course was exceptionally well attended and that some members of the congregation had joined together to form a Book Club. She informed the bishop that although this was in its very early stages it was already proving to be a huge success. (Jennie didn't know anything at all about the Book Club, but she thought that her comments sounded good.) 'What book are they discussing?'

'The Bible I think.' She replied quickly. She was just about to tell the bishop about the possibility of putting into practice Bryn's latest brainchild - converting the back of the church into a children's corner- when she heard the front door opening.

'We're in the kitchen,' she called, with a strong emphasis on the '*we*.'

She looked at the clock. It was almost a quarter past five. If Bryn was at all surprised to see his unexpected visitor, he certainly didn't show it.

'How good to see you, Father,' he exclaimed with respect. He glanced at the two remaining sandwiches. 'I see that Jennie has been looking after you.'

'Indeed, she has, Bryn. I don't know why, but I was absolutely *starving*! Not any more. I'm as full as an egg now.'

Jennie winced as he slapped his fat stomach to convey his satisfaction. Bryn sat on the empty chair next to Jennie and put his arm around her affectionately. He had realised much earlier in the day that he had double booked the evening's events, and had intended sending an e-mail to Bishop Anselm offering his apologies for absence as soon as he got home. He was just about to give a verbal apology instead when the bishop asked, 'Alright for a lift to Pont Gwallter this evening, please Bryn? As I explained to Jennie I came up with Dean Martin. He's gone to visit his daughter but I'll go back with him of course.'

Although Bryn expressed that he would be delighted to provide transport to the evening meeting his thoughts were very much focused on the fact that he would not be available to celebrate Jennie's retirement as planned. Just as he was pondering what to do next, Bishop Anselm requested that he and Bryn speak confidentially as he had several queries and questions to discuss.

'We'll go into the study,' said Bryn. 'Go ahead Father, you know the way. I'll be there in a moment.'

The bishop certainly knew the way, as he had been the previous incumbent at St. Mary Magdalene's prior to his election as Bishop. Maybe that is why he chose to take the tradesmen's entrance as opposed to ringing the bell at the front door. Over the years St. Mary Magdalene Rhydbrychan had been a prime parish within the diocese and a stepping stone to Archdeaconries and even to the occasional Bishopric. Bryn had been inducted into the parish about seven years earlier, shortly after Bishop Anselm's Enthronement. Jennie was becoming increasingly disillusioned with the Church in Wales. Bryn seemed to be overlooked when it came to promotions or recognition of a job well done. Surely Bishop Anselm could accommodate him as an Honorary Canon if nothing else. That would at least be a tangible 'thank you' for his unstinting and dedicated work in the diocese.

'I'm so sorry, Jen, So *very* sorry,' said Bryn quietly but with feeling, when he heard the bishop's footsteps on the wooden floor of the study. He explained how he had intended sending an e-mail to Anselm apologising for his absence from this evening's meeting but, when he saw him eating and drinking in their kitchen, he simply had to go along with archidiaconal plans. There was nothing he could do about it. His schedule that day had been particularly full, especially as the child protection meeting at St. Deiniol's Retreat House had far extended the predicted time of completion. This was partly due to the fact that half the members of the committee had arrived at 11 o'clock instead of 10 o'clock because of an oral blunder. The new chairperson of the group, the Reverend I.B. Savage, had misinformed those who had felt the need to telephone him in order to confirm the time of the meeting. 'The information that I am about to give you is off the top of my head,' he had said angrily to each caller. 'I can't seem to find the necessary documentation. I believe it begins at 11 o'clock.' In fact he had, instead, given the callers the time of the local school's Fairtrade Coffee Morning for which he had already sent his apologies. Jennie poured Bryn a cup of tea. 'We can celebrate another night. It really doesn't matter at all. I'm feeling a little bit on edge, so perhaps it's just as well. Take these sandwiches into the study with you. In view of the fact that the three large slices of chocolate sponge have been consumed, I'll cut another one. You'll need to eat something before you go out again. You haven't got much time.'

'Fortunately we had a good lunch at St. Deiniol's, but thanks, Jen and thank you for being so understanding.'

He gave her a quick kiss and went in to hear what confidentialities the bishop had to share. For a split second Jennie had the urge to hover outside the door of the study in an attempt to glean a little information regarding this, but immediately decided against it. As she placed the empty whisky glass in the dishwasher she thought that perhaps, at last, Bryn's moment had come and he was to be offered preferment of some kind. Maybe he would emerge from the study as an honorary canon or even as Bishop's Chaplain when he would be able to bring up the rear of every commanding and colourful episopal procession not only in the cathedral but throughout the diocese. Jennie was beginning to get excited. However, Bryn himself neither considered nor expected any sort of promotion. In fact he was a very humble person indeed. He was a dedicated priest and followed his vocation with love and devotion. He never wanted any thanks or acknowledgement for what he did, and nothing was ever too much for him. He always had time for everyone, especially those who were marginalised or on the fringe of society. The people of the parish, particularly the elderly and infirm, appreciated his regular visits. He seemed to put himself and his own needs last, even to the point of wrestling with chest infections and other ailments in order to complete his list of engagements. Jennie often reminded him that even God took a rest day, after a week of unstinting effort for others. As a man of the cloth he was steadfast and committed; as a man about the house he was caring, devoted and loyal. Jennie's mother- in- law had been completely accurate when she had said many years before 'My boy is one in a million!'

It was shortly after six o' clock when Bryn, closely followed by the bishop, came into the kitchen to tell Jennie that they were leaving for Pont Gwallter. Bryn told her that he hoped the meeting wouldn't go on for too long.

'Here! Here!' endorsed Bishop Anselm with gusto. 'I hope to get back to St. Deiniol's by 10 o'clock at the very latest or Gwenda's fish and chip shop will be closed. Already I fancy a cod in batter and mushy peas. Oh, and a large portion of chips of course, and a thick slice of fresh bread with lashings of butter.'

He slapped his stomach again and gave a broad grin. Jennie hated the way he did that; she thought it was so unbecoming, and surely it was the bread of heaven that he should be more concerned about! Jennie went to the front door to wave them off to the all important meeting. She was able to work out in record time the fact that if Bryn had been given a penny for every meeting that he had attended during his ministry - be it all-important, important, or not even important at all - then they could have taken an Alaskan cruise or purchased themselves an ISA.

She made a cup of coffee and sat at the kitchen table deep in thought. How was she going to spend her time this evening? After all, she was likely to retire only once in her lifetime and that time had come; it was upon her in the here and now. Jennie had a choice of three options - she could go along to the Gala Bingo that was organised by the local Derby and Joan Club and held in the church hall on the last Friday of the month; on the other hand she could turn up at the W.I. that met every Friday in the village hall and beg if she could join up there and then; or she could concentrate on writing some of the many thank you letters that she needed to see to. She decided on the latter and went into the study to get a packet of notelets that had been specially produced in aid of parish funds. On the front of the card was a magnificent picture of the church of St. Mary Magdalene with its towering spire and beautifully maintained grounds. Although the cards had only been available for a few weeks almost £100 had been raised. Bryn had already made enquiries regarding souvenir tea towels and ballpoint pens as a means of additional income for the parish.

Jennie returned to the kitchen table and sat down. She decided that her first letter of thanks would be to the family of Rhys Morris. As she had walked along the corridor towards her classroom on the previous Monday morning, she had seen Mrs. Morris waiting outside with Rhys in tow. Jennie had assumed that Mrs. Morris had come to complain that Rhys was being bullied by Jonathan again, but Jennie had observed no evidence of this over the past few weeks. When she got a little closer to them she could see that Mrs. Morris was giving her a toothless smile, 'ow-be love? We're sorry you're going.'

'Come into the classroom for a minute Mrs. Morris. It's nice to see you.'

Mother and son followed her into the music and drama studio. Jennie could see that the visit was going to be more amicable than she had first thought. However, she was gob smacked when Mrs. Morris removed two beautifully wrapped gifts from her 'bag for life,' one adorned with a pink rosette and the other with a blue one.

'You open the pink one, Miss,' Rhys had said eagerly. 'The blue one's for your 'usband.'

Jennie had felt quite emotional as she opened the gift; this family found it difficult to make ends meet at the best of times and they could ill-afford to spend their money on others. Tears came to her eyes and she was glad that the rest of the class was still in the playground. She removed the packaging carefully, with the intention of recycling the paper. Her retirement gift from this little family was a frozen chicken dinner for one.

'Your 'usband 'ave got the same,' said Rhys quickly. 'Let 'im open it 'imself Miss.'

'I will indeed Rhys. He will be thrilled with this I know. Thank you so much Mrs. Morris. This was so *very, very* kind of you,' said Jennie with feeling.

'You're welcome love; you've done a good job with our Rhys and our Andrew before 'im, not to mention Michelle, the little devil. 'ow you coped with 'er I'll never know, but 'ere she is now working part-time in the 'ospital. It's all thanks to you love.'

With that Mrs. Morris brought another package out of her bag. 'I 'aven't wrapped this up love. It's just a bit of extra Smash for the dinner incase your 'usband 'ave got a big appetite. Them factories don't put much tater on them plates of roast dinner. When I do buy these dinners for us on a Christmas I do put a whole tin of peas on Malc's and 'e do still want more. I got to go now love. I got an 'ospital appointment at 'a' past nine. All the very best and thank you love. I'ope the next bugger ....er...teacher will be as nice as you.'

'Thank you Mrs. Morris. Take care.'

Jennie and Rhys had taken the gifts over to the home economics room where they could be stored in the freezer until the end of the day. That had been the first of many an emotional moment for Jennie as her retirement had drawn closer.

She wrote several more cards including one to the members of the school choir, thanking them not only for the generous gifts but also for their dedication and commitment to the Brynglas Choir over the years. They had performed superbly at every concert, but their recent appearance on the Fantasy Stage at Disneyland Paris had been a particularly memorable experience for her and for the children too, of course. For most of them it had been the trip of a lifetime as few of her pupils were able to partake of a family holiday. Financial difficulties and limitations meant that many of them remained within the perimeter of their own localities during the school holidays.

Jennie enclosed a special thank you card for Ieuan, Emma's father, who had accompanied them on many of their engagements, in order to record the events for fun and for posterity, and she expressed how much she was looking forward to watching the DVD of these events in the days to come. She also wrote to a number of parents who had 'clubbed together' to present her with a specially made wooden love spoon complete with a treble clef, a celtic cross and daffodils. She thought that it was really remarkable. At that point Jennie thought that she would take a break and go upstairs to put on her slippers. After all, she had been wearing these black patent high heel shoes, though not as high as those worn by Miss Wilkins, for the best part of twelve hours, apart from when she was exercising in the kitchen, and they could hardly be described as the most comfortable of footwear. As Jennie sat on the chaise-longue she decided that, instead of merely changing her shoes, she would take a bath. For more than half an hour she relaxed in the oil of primrose, complete with candle that had kindly been given to her by the domestic staff. The magnificent basket of bath oils, shower gel, soaps and moisturisers would see her well into the following year; along with the many other toiletries she had been given.

After what Jennie considered to be the most relaxing bath of all time, she put on her nightgown and bath robe and decided to go and watch television for a little while before turning in. The bath had done her good. She was feeling less stressed and much more on an even keel, as it were. She skipped down the stairs and opened the door of the sitting-room. As soon as she walked in a brilliant bouquet of flowers caught her eye. There was an arrangement of two dozen red roses on the coffee table and the accompanying card read…..'To my most wonderful wife as she retires from her beloved Brynglas. Here's to twenty five years of dedicated service to staff and pupils alike. Their loss is my gain!! All my love, Bryn. Xxxxxxxxx'

Jennie went to sit in the armchair. She was absolutely stunned. This was all too much for her; she had fought back tears for the best part of a week but now she just allowed them to come, and she cried and cried and cried. She wasn't crying because she had retired and she felt that life was passing her by; she was crying because she felt so deeply touched by the genuine love and affection that had been shown to her by so very many people. She reflected on the many gifts that she had been given to mark her retirement ranging from nutritious frozen dinners to the fragile statue of the Virgin Mary; from the magnificent display of toiletries to the small bottle of shampoo; from the grand floral arrangements to the garden greenery held together by toilet tissue; from the enormous boxes of chocolates to the bar of chocolate, the half bottle of flavoured water, the apple, the packet of crisps, the stick of chewing gum…and so much more… each and every gift had been given with love and as a token of gratitude.

Jennie was completely overcome by humility and emotion. She felt unworthy of such fondness and reward. As she wept she bowed her head in prayer and gave thanks to God that her profession had enabled her to meet so many wonderful people - colleagues, contemporaries, advisers and lecturers in the field of education but, above all, the parents and the pupils themselves. She would cherish the memories for ever.

In time she composed herself and thought that perhaps some Kenyan ground coffee would assist her present state of mind. She slapped her thigh, saying, 'No more nonsense,' and began to make her way into the kitchen. She looked at her watch. It was a quarter to nine. She thought that it wouldn't be too long before Bryn would be home; she would put enough coffee in the percolator for them both to have at least two cups each. Just as she was filling the kettle with water the door bell rang. This was unusual for a Friday night, particularly at this time. Before she had replaced the kettle on the worktop the bell rang again. Jennie hurried through the hallway and, being aware of her night attire, cautiously opened the front door. It was Selwyn Harrison.

'I need to see Bryn and I need him *now*!' he exclaimed anxiously. Selwyn was a frequent visitor to the vicarage. Bryn had befriended him since the time that he had collapsed on the vicarage drive as a result of a drug overdose some four years earlier. At that time in his life he had been of no fixed abode but, as a result of Bryn's determined endeavours, he had eventually been granted council accommodation on the estate in Rhydbrychan. His one bedroomed flat was kept in immaculate condition, and he invited Bryn and Jennie to his home for coffee and biscuits at least once every month. As soon as Jennie opened the door to him she could smell alcohol on his breath, and the way in which he was swaying from side to side confirmed that he had been drinking much more alcohol in one evening than that recommended by medics and health officials as a whole week's consumption!

'I want to see Bryn!' he repeated, sounding more aggressive 'and I want to see him *now!*'

'*Do come in* Selwyn,' said Jennie. 'Bryn isn't here at the moment but I'm expecting him any minute now.'

She escorted him to the armchair in the kitchen where he sat down with a thump. Jennie had had many dealings with Selwyn during the past four years and she recognised his greatest attribute as being non-violent. He could shout and scream and raise his voice but he would never raise his hand or his arm. His aggression began and ended with his vocal chords. 'Would you like a cup of tea Selwyn?' she asked.

'Uh? Whassat?' he asked. He was obviously not in tune to what Jennie was saying.

'I'll make you a cup of tea Selwyn.'

'No fanks. Don't bover. Gor a cold beer or a strong cider?'

'Sorry Selwyn, we're waiting for deliveries.'

'OK then. I'll have a cuppa wiv seven sugars.' He was slurring his words by now. 'Seven... my lucky number. Did you know vat ver world was made in seven days? You can read all about it in ver Bible Shennie. You can nick one from the back of the church. *I* did! There's plenty there. They 'ont miss one or two. Have a gander at 'em seven days, whar it says. It starts on page one I fink'.... and with that he fell fast asleep. Jennie just left him there and went into the sitting room to watch the television. She knew that Bryn wouldn't be too much longer and, after all, Selwyn considered himself to be almost part of the family. However, it was some time later when Jennie heard Bryn's car coming up the driveway, so she went to the front door to welcome him home - and to warn him about their unexpected visitor.

'Hi Jen!' he called as he locked the car. 'Sorry I've been so long but the meeting seemed to go on and on. Anyway it looks as though All Saints will have to be demolished. It's falling apart at the seams it seems! It has to close as of now!' He walked in through the front door and gave her a kiss. 'I'm surprised to see that you are still up. You shouldn't have waited for me. I thought that perhaps you would have had an early night. You must be exhausted. You go on up to bed. I'll be up straight behind you.' Bryn closed the front door, 'At least you can have a lie-in in the morning.'

'Indeed I shall Bryn. Anyway, you've got someone waiting to see you. At the moment he's in the kitchen sleeping off his evening's booze, but I'm sure he'll wake up when he hears your voice. He was really uptight on arrival, but settled down quite quickly. I'll give you three guesses as to who I'm referring.'

'I only need the one Jennie.' He walked towards the kitchen and in a loud voice called, 'Selwyn, my boy. How are you doing? Nice to see you, to see you, nice, but it's getting late.' Selwyn woke up with a start. He was somewhat disorientated, 'Hey, Bryn. Good to see you mate. What you doing here ven?'

'I live here Selwyn,' Bryn replied.

'Ugh?' replied Selwyn sleepily. He sat up, rubbed his eyes and looked around. 'By damn, you're right. Vis is your house not mine. I can't remember why I came, but I'd better be on my way now.' He squinted at the kitchen clock. 'Look at ve time. It's quarter to 'leven. No offence, mate, but I'd better be off. Hope you don't mind.'

As Selwyn stood up to go Bryn could see that he seemed very unsteady on his feet. He veered to left and right, fell back and slumped into the armchair. Bryn moved towards him to offer assistance.

Selwyn tried again. 'It's OK mate. Stand back. I can do it.'

Fortunately the second attempt was more successful but even so Bryn remained concerned. Because Selwyn's flat was a good ten minutes walk from the vicarage he offered to give him a lift home by car. 'You don't have to do vat but fanks, mate. I'm feeling a bit shaky, like I've got a cold coming on or summat,' said Selwyn as he lurched through the hallway towards the front door. 'And be sure to say hello from me to vat *lovely, beautiful, sharmin'* lady of yours. Sorry I missed her.'

Selwyn almost fell into the passenger seat of Bryn's three door Citroen, cracking his head on the roof of the car as he went, then he slammed the door shut. 'Home James!' he said as he ruffled Bryn's ginger curls and then laughed uncontrollably for some time. After he had paused for breath he sang 'Oh what a night!!' time and time again.

Bryn was relieved when he turned the car into Heol Dewi Sant and pulled up outside number twenty seven. 'I'll come in with you if you like Selwyn. Do you want any help to find your pyjamas or any thing?'

'No fanks mate. Just me and my boxers tonight. Chow!' and with that he slammed the car door and staggered up the short garden path that led to his ground floor flat.

Bryn waited until he saw the light go on in Selwyn's living room before turning on the ignition. Only then did he feel sufficiently at ease to leave Selwyn to his own devices.

When Bryn returned home he went straight upstairs to join Jennie. He apologised again for letting her down, as he put it, regarding the celebration dinner. She explained that a night in, on her own for the most part, had done her good and she told Bryn that she had had a chance to sort herself out and get some correspondence written. She told him that, on the whole, the evening had been fruitful, relaxing and peaceful and how she had been completely overwhelmed by the magnificent bouquet of red roses. 'And what about you?' she asked. 'It's such a shame about All Saints.'

'Nick the Vic was devastated as you can imagine, but Bishop Anselm pointed out that St. Twrog's church is less than four hundred yards down the same road albeit in the opposite direction, and to have two churches in one street neither of which was full to bursting even at Festivals, was absolutely unnecessary in this day and age. He said that it was time for the parish to move forward. Most of us thought that it was the only way to go.'

'It doesn't make any difference to me, but you're home later than I expected. I hope that Bishop Anselm will get to Gwenda's fish bar before it closes or he'll be more devastated than Nick the Vic!'

'No problem on that front Jennie,' replied Bryn as he got into bed. 'At about 9:30 he asked to borrow my mobile, and I heard him giving his order to Gwenda and asking her to leave it on her garden bench in the back if he wasn't back before closing time. He said he could easily warm it up in the microwave and if there was anything going waste to include it in the order.'

'I'm beginning to loose patience with that man. He needs to move into the twenty-first century,' said Jennie. 'Only two things are needful. A mobile phone and a driving license. He has neither and expects the pickings of both. He depends too much on the kindness and good-will of others.'

Bryn turned out the light and snuggled up to Jennie. They both had had an exhausting day and were ready to go to sleep. Jennie was mulling over the last week of employment and Bryn was thinking about the meeting and the implications it would have for both incumbent and parishioners.

'Goodnight my love,' said Jennie, 'Guess where I'm having supper tomorrow evening…down Yr Hen Efail. Fancy coming?'

'I'll be there before you. I'll save you a seat. I can't wait to celebrate your retirement, can you?'

'In a manner of speaking I already have. Goodnight and God bless.'

The Vicarage was taken over by silence and tranquillity and all was well; they may even have called to mind the words of St. Julian of Norwich – 'All will be well, all will be well, all manner of things shall be well.' Bryn and Jennie had much to look forward to in the days and years ahead as a new chapter of their lives was about to begin.

Chapter 2:
NO PEACE FOR THE WICKED?

BRRR
BRRR
Beep-Beep
Beep. Beep

Jennie awoke suddenly in response to the shrill sound of the alarm clock. It was six thirty. 'Time to get up already', she thought to herself as she leaned over to turn it off. As she did so she realised that today wasn't a working day after all; in fact her dedication to duty had come to an end the day before and from now on Jennie would have all the time in the world to do what she wanted and when she wanted. She was now a lady of leisure. Therefore Jennie was annoyed that she had not adjusted the automatic alarm the night before, but old habits die hard and she had been reliant on its services since the day that it had been purchased.

Jennie moved herself into a recovery position to get over the unnecessary trauma and began to enjoy what she planned to be a long and restful lie-in. At that point Bryn came into the room carrying coffee in a mug that had been awarded to the 'World's Greatest Teacher'. It was one of the presents from her school choir and was being used for the very first time. 'Don't spill. You look half asleep. Why didn't you switch off the alarm? Are you thinking of taking an early morning jog or something?'

'Human error,' she replied.

'Do you have any plans today?' asked Bryn.

'I have one plan today, and one plan only; that is to do absolutely nothing for the whole of the day, apart perhaps from reading the book that you gave me for my birthday. I intend to enjoy the ambience of my own home for a change.' She sipped her coffee and began to relax. 'What are your plans today?' she asked. 'I know you told me, but I seem to have forgotten.'

'I have the meeting at St. Deiniol's from 10:00 until 4:00. It begins with a 9:30 Eucharist, so I thought I'd leave here around seven as I've arranged to pick up Dai Trent on the way.'

'On the way!' Jennie gasped in disbelief. 'It must be a good ten miles *out* of your way. He could have arranged to meet you in Llanmaldwyn at the very least.'

'It seems that Ann has an early appointment at the hairdresser's and she needs the car, otherwise, he said that he would have been glad to give me a lift to the meeting this time.'

'If you believe that you'll believe anything. You're too willing, Bryn. You're going to wear yourself out. I know that I told the children in school to say 'No' to strangers, but I'm advising you to say 'No' to colleagues sometimes. You do too much and you need a break.'

'I'm going to sort out a holiday for us in the next few days and that's a cub promise, as he saluted and said most enthusiastically and convincingly, '*Dib! Dib! Dib! Dob! Dob! Dob!*' He gave a boyish hop, skip and jump. 'We both need a change Jen. I've arranged to have two Sundays off at the end of the August. Tom Collins is covering the first Sunday and Dai Trent the second one. Where would you like to go? What about the Costa Del Barry Island? Ha! Ha!'

'Somewhere where it's hot and sunny Bryn and where we can sit on a balcony and look at the sea; somewhere where I can have you all to myself, so if Dai Trent's helping you out with services I hope he doesn't need a lift, particularly if we holiday abroad. In that case most of the vacation will be taken up transporting Dai Trent. I'm sorry if I sound a bit unkind at the moment, but I really think you're overdoing things, Bryn. You need to sit back and take stock. So many of your contemporaries sit back without taking stock or taking anything else apart from time out! End of speech. Have a good day and give my love to Dai Trent. Give 'us' a kiss before you go. Just think, love, we'll have so much more time for things like this now that I've retired. I will be around 24:7, so who's a lucky boy then?'

They enjoyed a passionate moment together before Bryn made a move.

'You relax and enjoy. Remember, this is a special day for you; a day when you can do your own thing in your own time, without having to respond to the needs of others.'

Having given Jennie a final kiss, he returned to the study to collect the documents that he required for the meeting and to deal with some urgent correspondence that needed posting. When Jennie had finished drinking her coffee she snuggled under the duvet and went back to sleep. It was 9:45 a.m. when she awoke again. She felt calm and well rested and reached over to the bedside cabinet for her book. It was called 'Little Red Posies' by U.R. White, a rather unique combination between title and author, but it had received good reviews in several of the leading newspapers.

She put on her reading glasses and lay back on the pillow. The sun was shining through the east window, so there was no need for artificial light.

The heading below Chapter One said 'Blessings'. She looked towards the window and thought how very blessed she herself was. She had a wonderful husband, a comfortable home, she was part of a prayerful but active parish and, above all, she expected this day, as quoted in Psalm 122, to provide 'peace within her walls'.

Just as her eyes returned to the print the doorbell gave its piercing reverberation. She had suggested to Bryn some years before that they changed the sound of the bell to a hymn tune, perhaps even that of 'Onward Christian Pilgrims' (alias 'Onward Christian Soldiers'), but he said that if the piercing ring was good enough for his predecessor then it was good enough for him. As she quickly donned her Disneyland dressing gown the doorbell rang again. Bryn frequently received packages that were too large and bulky to go through the letter box, so Jennie assumed that it was the postman making a delivery.

'Coming!' she called as she hurried down the stairs. 'Just a moment.'

'Good morning,' she said pleasantly as she opened the door, expecting to be handed something from Royal Mail. It was, instead, Mrs. Lillian Shanks. Lillian invariably seemed to have an air of superiority about her and often rubbed people up the wrong way. On the other hand she was a regular worshipper, a dedicated member of the Mothers' Union and an active member of the Parochial Church Council. She was always prepared to air her views at meetings, even though her remarks were not always well received.

'Is the Vicar in, dear?' she enquired, casually observing that Jennie was still wearing her night attire. 'You might think that it's a bit early but there's something *very* important that I need to discuss with him.'

'I'm afraid he's not Lillian, but, *do come in* and maybe I can help.'

'Are you sure it is convenient, dear?' she asked as she walked with confidence straight into the study and sat in the large armchair to the right of Bryn's old oak desk. She had been here before!

Jennie sat on Bryn's office chair and rotated it somewhat nervously, wishing that she had already showered and dressed herself.

'It's about the Harvest Supper dear,' said Mrs. Shanks.

She paused, waiting for a response from Jennie who, at the time, was making a mental calculation. It would be a good two and a half months before the Harvest Supper. Had she hurried downstairs in her nightdress, just to hear about this?

Lillian Shanks continued. 'I was wondering about the possibility of a change of dessert this year. We've been serving apple tarts as dessert ever since I came here and that's nearly thirty years ago.' Mrs. Lillian Shanks had moved from Bakewell in Yorkshire when her husband Lambert had been appointed Manager of Rhydbrychan Abbatoir, and during this time he had had been affectionately known as Lam Shanks, the Abbatoir. They had lived in the old school house which was only a short walk from the church and had been warmly welcomed into the parish of St. Mary Magdalene.

Within a short space of time, they had both become active members of several church organizations. Lillian became Chair of the fabric committee and Lambert took on the role of Sacristan. It was at the time that he was people's warden, however, that he suffered a brain haemorrhage and died suddenly, shortly after returning from a holiday in Egypt.

Lillian always maintained that his sudden and premature death was due to the fact that he had done a belly crawl through one of the pyramids in complete darkness, in order to see an original tomb. Whilst making a brief but emotional statement at the reception following the funeral service, she thanked everyone for their prayers and their support and expressed that she had no intention of returning to Yorkshire. She had found earth's Promised Land right here in Rhydbrychan.

'Apple tart is traditional I suppose,' said Jennie.

'It's time for a change, my dear,' replied Lillian ardently. 'I propose that we serve pear pies instead. There's equal goodness in pears and they are one and the same of 'all God's gifts around us.' As you know, we see them side by side on the window displays at Harvest Festivals. What do you think, my dear?'

'Well, I..er…'

'And another thing,' interrupted Lillian. "Dwynwen Morris has gone in for surgery today. Did the Vicar know that? I don't think it's anything serious, but I'm sure that he'd want to visit. Perhaps you would inform him, dear. But back to the pear pies. What do you think?'

'It sounds a nice idea, but how would the ladies feel about making pear pies instead of apple tarts?'

Jennie couldn't believe that she was discussing Harvest Supper menus in mid- July, and especially on this, her first day of retirement. She immediately began to wonder if she had done the right thing in taking early retirement. Only a few days before, one of her colleagues had suggested that Jennie might find that she had time on her hands until she adjusted to retirement. After all, she was experiencing a milestone in her life.

'I'll have a word with Bryn about it when he comes home this evening,' said Jennie.

At this point Jennie expected Mrs. Shanks to begin to make a move; after all, she had said her piece and had been assured that it would be looked into. Instead, however, Lillian crossed her legs and appeared to be making herself more comfortable.

'By the way, dear' - she invariably called people 'dear'. (However, she always addressed Bryn as 'Vicar' and maybe due to the Yorkshire lilt it seemed that Bishop Anselm was always 'an'some!) 'By the way dear,' she repeated, 'did you know that people have been viewing the property next door? I thought you may be interested since whoever makes the purchase will be your neighbours. I hope they reduced the price. I'm given to understand that it requires a great deal of renovation. I can't see anyone moving in for years.'

At that moment the telephone rang. Jennie was sitting close enough to the desk to answer it immediately. As far as Jennie was concerned Lillian was beginning to outstay her welcome, so she quickly decided to ham it up a bit. 'Top of the morning. You have been connected to Rhydbrychan Vicarage. Jennie Jenkins, the Vicar's better half speaking, *so,* how can I help?'

There was a prolonged silence as Jennie listened to whoever was at the other end of the line. In a loud whisper, intending to arouse the interest of her visitor, though at the same time implying secrecy, she asked the caller, 'Is that common knowledge? Does everyone who should know about it *really* know about it, if you see what I mean?'

The conversation continued with a few *oohs!!* and *aahhs!!* from Jennie, then a long pause followed. Lillian noticed that Jennie appeared to be shaking her head as though she was hearing something poignant, so she strained to hear what was being said, but it was to no avail.

'So it's one o' clock from the house.'

Another long pause followed as Jennie listened to what the caller had to say. During this time Lillian thought she saw Jennie wipe a tear from her eye as she appeared to nod her head compassionately. Then, '*Ha! Ha! Ha!*' she suddenly hooted. 'I've been expecting this for a long time. *Ha! Ha! Ha!*' Jennie put down the receiver and continued to laugh almost uncontrollably. 'A time like this, and we've been asked to dress incognito. I can't believe it!'

'It seems to me that you are behaving most inappropriately if you don't mind my saying so, dear.'

'What do you mean, Lillian?' asked Jennie in surprise.

'Well, I couldn't help but hear at least part of the conversation dear, and it sounded to me as though you were making funeral arrangements. When you went on to laugh at the top of your voice I thought it was quite out of order, if you don't mind my saying so dear. I don't think that the vicar would be very impressed at all.'

'Lillian, the caller was a friend of mine, who will be picking me up at one o'clock from the house here on Tuesday of next week to go to a college reunion.'

Jennie couldn't believe that she was relaying her personal telephone call to Mrs. Shanks, so she decided to say no more.

'I'm sorry dear, but I assumed that you were taking a message from the undertaker and I considered your response to be completely improper. Well, I think I ought to be getting along if you don't mind. Please would you convey my message to the vicar as a matter of urgency?'

With that, she stood up, raised her right arm at a forty five degree angle, comparable to that displayed by a notorious personality of the Forties, and prepared to leave. 'Pear pies or no pear pies? - that is the question,' she shouted as she walked towards the front door. 'Good bye dear'. On that note Lillian Shanks left the premises.

Jennie had to make a very quick decision. She really needed a cup of coffee to recover from Lillian's visit, but there was always the possibility of another caller and she didn't want to get caught in her Disneyland attire for a second time that morning. Anyway, she decided to take the risk, and went into the kitchen to switch the kettle on.

Unfortunately for her, even before the water had boiled, the doorbell rang again. She was in two minds whether to answer it or not, but she knew that she could never forgive herself if someone was to be left wanting, so she hurried to the door and opened it in a manner that only her head could be seen. She was proud of such a successful manoeuvre.

'Reverend home?' enquired a large burly man, clad in what can only be described as a boiler suit. It was a kind of garden green colour. 'Got an appointment at 2:30.'

Jennie wondered why on earth Bryn had arranged an appointment for a time that he knew that he would not be available. She hoped that he wasn't becoming confused as he had years of first class ministry left in him. And why had this husky hunk of a fellow arrived so early for an afternoon appointment?

'Sorry, lady. Let me introduce myself. I'm Ray... Gardener.'

'I'm very pleased to meet you Mr. Gardener,' replied Jennie politely as she spoke through the narrow gap between the door and the lintel.

'I'm not Mr. Gardener. I'm a Jones. Ray Jones of 'Grounds and Gardens'.

As Jennie unwittingly opened the door a little Ray caught a glimpse of Winnie the Pooh on the front of her dressing gown. 'Don't tell me. I've dragged you out of bed. What's up? Dose of flu? There's a lot of it going around at the moment.'

Jennie was beginning to feel uncomfortable and went on to explain that Bryn wasn't expected home until much later and would therefore be unable to keep the appointment.

'Now then. Neither can I!' replied Ray. 'It's like this you see Mrs. Vicar.' He paused. 'I hope you don't mind me calling you that.' She did mind, very much indeed in fact, but there was no way that she wanted to enter into a discussion with Grounds and Gardens at the present time.

'It's like this,' continued Ray. 'Your better half - or is he? *Ha! Ha!*- asked me to start work here today at 2:30, but that old, snooty Miss Cox at Pengarnddu insists that I cut the hedges and clear the brambles A.S.A.P. It was only lawn mowing to start with but now she wants the whole caboose. To cut a long story short I need more time at Pengarnddu.'

'You take as long as you like, Mr. Jones. We're in no rush here.'

'I'm not so sure, Mrs. Vicar. There's a hell.....oh pardon me!...there's a lot of work needing doing here love. Anyway, I'll be on the blower to your boss. Cheers!'

Ray Jones left the vicarage, but with a firm intention to return before too long. After all, a garden this size could bring in enough beer money to last him for the rest of the year at least.

Jennie closed the door and took a deep breath before racing upstairs. She was determined to have a shower and get dressed before anyone else dropped by. As the warm water sprayed over her body, she began to unwind and she was able to erase both the visit of Lillian Shanks and that of Ray Jones completely from her mind. The smell of her newly acquired shower gel was like nectar to the bees. She reminded herself that this was to be a day for her, and her alone, and from here-on in she was going to enjoy the tranquillity of her own company and the ambience of her own home.

She was oblivious to the fact that during her time in the bathroom, the telephone had rung three times in quick succession. Jennie dressed casually but neatly in black trousers and a pink cotton top. Winnie the Pooh and Friends were nowhere to be seen. She returned to the kitchen to percolate a pot of coffee; this was the only sound that she wanted to hear at present. Her 'Little Pink Posies' had been placed on the kitchen table so that she could continue to read the first chapter. As soon as the coffee was ready she filled her mug and hollered '*Salute! Cheers! Iechyd Da! Here's to me!*' She proceeded to nod her head in various directions as though there were others present, and then smiled benignly as she sat down and opened her book and began to read. '*It was a miserable night in more ways than one when Mrs. Ferguson arrived at the hospital. She knew all too well what to expect. Those lazy, crazy days of Summer had given way to a Winter of discontent for the whole family. The reason for this was....*' A piercing ring of the doorbell caused Jennie to lose concentration. As she walked towards the door, a second ring, much longer than the first one, greeted her ears. 'Just a moment,' she called courteously, though under her breath she was commanding the visitor not to be so damned impatient. She opened the door, only to behold yet another boiler suit; this one was as white as snow and its occupier was of similar colour. As Jennie took a second glance at this whiter shade of pale she noticed what seemed to be a pair of chef's trousers peeping through a large tear in the material. For a brief moment she wondered if he was making a home delivery.

'Morning Missus, or is it afternoon yet? Mark Strencham, Billings Alarms. I was here this time last year. Your old man let me in.'

'I wasn't expecting anyone to check the alarm system today,' replied Jennie.

'My fault entirely, Missus. I'm trying to kill two birds with one stone like. I've just done St. Stephen's Lwff-y-dwlb, so I dropped in by 'ere on the way back. Called on the off chance you might say. It'll save me coming back in a few weeks. Somebody told me you're due on the seventh.'

Jennie glanced down to her stomach, wondering if there was something that Mark Strencham knew about, of which she herself was completely uninformed.

'*Do come in* Mr. Strencham and do what you have to do.'

'OK Missus. Don't mind me. You carry on as if I wasn't here.' But, with all the beeping and screeching that was to follow, this was indeed a most absurd remark. Mark Strencham made his way to the loft where his endeavours were to take place.

'Lovely smell of coffee Missus,' he called from the landing, but Jennie chose to have a spasm of selective hearing loss at this point. She quickly downed the contents of her mug and placed it in the dishwashing machine. She was wondering what was best to do next - empty the dryer or check that her flowers had enough water - when she heard a strident *Beep! Beep! Beep! Beep!* followed by a shrill *Brrrrrrrrrrrrrrr*! that was repeated again and again over at least a five minute period. Then silence prevailed. Jennie assumed that 'Billings Alarms' had finished the assessment. She was immediately proved to be wrong; the most penetrating screech that she had ever heard was to follow....*Eeeeeeeeeeeeeeeeeeee!!!Beep!... Beep!Beep!...Beep! Beep! Beep! Beep! Bee...eeep!!...Fftt!!... Fftt!... Beep!Beep!.....Brrrrrrrrrrrrrr! Eeeeeeeeeeeeeeeeee!!!* It was repeated no less than half a dozen times. Shortly after the final chord a voice called down from the loft.

'Nearly finished! I've just got to go through it all once more to double check. I can't take any risks or I'll lose my job.'

Jennie covered her ears and shook her head in dismay. It seemed like an eternity before the task was complete.

'All done and everything's working perfectly,' Mark Strencham called as he made his way downstairs and into the kitchen. 'I said it's all done now and everything is working perfectly. To tell you the truth Missus I could see almost from the start that there weren't any problems, but I had to cover my back!' Fortunately he made no further reference to the lovely aroma of coffee. 'I'll be on my bike now, Missus. See you next year.'

'Surely the Diocese doesn't expect you to pedal from place to place Mr. Strencham?' said Jennie with certain sarcasm.

'Figure of speech, Missus. I've got my Jag parked by 'ere. Brand new too and with my personalised number plate, see.'

Jennie followed him out to the forecourt and read GR 8 MK.

'Do you agree with that?' he asked as he got into the car, but he didn't wait for an answer.

He toot - tooted the horn, waved and then drove off, satisfied that he had managed to kill two birds with one stone and cover his back at the same time, even without cutting corners!

It was well past mid-day when Jennie went into the study to go to the computer to check her e-mails. As she walked towards Bryn's desk she noticed that the light on the answering machine was flashing. She always listened in to any recorded messages incase Bryn was needed urgently and she could explain that he was unavailable at that moment in time. She pressed the green light and sat down.

'Hello Vicar. Meirion Lloyd here. Just to let you know that I won't be in church on Sunday to read the Old Testament lesson. I think that Jan Bevan is down to read the New.... so maybe she'll do both. Thanks. Bye for now.'

As the light continued to flash, the next message came on. 'Hi Vicar. This is Jan Bevan. Something's cropped up so I won't be there on Sunday to read the New Testament lesson. I know that Meirion is down to read the Old... so I'm sure that he wouldn't mind reading the two. See you soon. Hwyl!'

The light continued to flash for the third message. 'Good morning Vicar. Pat Lewis here. I meant to ring last night. I've been invited down to Devon for the weekend, so I won't be there to play the organ on Sunday. I know that in the past both Jan Bevan and Meirion Lloyd have been prepared to help out with the church music, so at least you have a choice of accompanists. One is as good as the other, so perhaps you'll want to take their names out of your biretta! Bye -ee!' End of messages.

Jennie picked up the receiver and spoke in a deafening voice. 'Hello! Hello! And *again* I say Hello! Harken all ye parishioners of St. Mary Magdalene, Rhydbrychan, in the Diocese of St. Deiniol's. If ye have ears to hear then, for my brethren and companion's sake listen up! This is no joke buddies. If at any time, you discover that you are unable to carry out a duty to which you have been assigned, be it organ playing, serving at the altar, readings, intercessions, etcettera, etcettera, etcettera would you please arrange for substitutes yourselves!!' She replaced the receiver, grabbed the church keys from the key rack and, knowing that the role of organist for Sunday's service would be assigned to yours truly, she made her way over to the church to practice the hymns that had been chosen for the Sunday morning Eucharist.

As she walked down the church path, she could see that the church door was already open. She felt that the Lord's invitation of '*Do Come In*' was a far more sincere salutation than the welcome that she had been offering that day. Jennie closed the door quietly behind her and walked in in silence. There was always that million to one chance that someone might be on their knees in prayer. As she looked towards the altar she could see May and Helen putting the finishing touches to the floral arrangement in the sanctuary. She strolled slowly up the aisle.

'What a beautiful arrangement,' exclaimed Jennie as she approached the organ. 'Where would we be without you?'

May and Helen were pillars of the parish of St. Mary Magdalene and were completely supportive of the Vicar and all that he attempted to arrange. In fact, they were friends of everyone and respected by all. They were real life doers and not hearers only.

'Hello Jennie,' said Helen. 'I didn't expect to see you here today. Isn't this the first day of retirement? If I were you I would have spent the day enjoying the ambience of my own home and perhaps reading a book and drinking coffee.

What brings you here, sojourner? - Dickens or Shakespeare? - or maybe it was neither of the two. Anyway, it sounds like a familiar quote.'

'What brings me here, Helen, is that all our organists have all taken their annual leave at the same time, though not, as far as I am aware, in the same place.'

May, who had not been listening to the conversation in its entirety, had picked up the fact that Jennie had come along to practice the hymns for Sunday.

'I thought that Pat looked pale and peaky in Mothers' Union. She's not going down under is she?'

'Not quite as far as that May. It seems that she's going to Devon for the weekend,' replied Jennie. 'I think she has family there.' May and Helen began to pick up the greenery that they had dropped around the floral arrangement. They were preparing to leave.

'Hey guys!' Jennie called from the organ bench. 'Any chance of you doing the readings on Sunday morning?' and before they had time to answer she said, 'Thanks a bunch. I know that I can always depend on you.'

She went on to stress that there was no mention of Roaboam or Jeroaboam in the Old Testament reading. On one occasion, at an evening service held in the not too distant past, May had found extreme difficulty in delivering the narrative regarding these two Old Testament figures, and she had vowed never to read this passage of Scripture aloud in church again. She had got into such a knot with the names that she had succumbed to laughter as she stood at the lectern reading the lesson. She had apologised and started again, only to end up with another chuckle each time she mentioned their names. She preferred to read from the Acts of the Apostles.

'It seems as though our organist and assigned readers are all away at the same time. You'll find where the readings are from on last week's newsletter. I must get down to business now; no peace for the wicked,' said Jennie, pulling out two of the five organ stops. 'Before you go, what's your opinion on pear pies?'

'If you steep the pears in red wine overnight it should be OK,' replied Helen. 'Otherwise I think they would be bland and rather tasteless. Cheerio Jennie, we'll leave you to it. All I hope is, that we haven't got 'For All the Saints' on Sunday. It leaves me completely knackered, pardon the expression.'

May and Helen took one last look at the arrangements and, feeling satisfied, left for home. Jennie had the place to herself, apart from the eternal presence of the Lord. He took her for what she was, and was conscious of all her faults, so without further ado she pulled out all five organ stops and played a magnificent rendition of Beethoven's 'Ode to Joy' by means of a warm up. This was indeed a very basic organ; although it didn't have foot pedals, it was amazing what sounds Jennie, and others, got out of it.

Having finished the voluntary on a high, she proceeded to consult the list of hymns that had been chosen for the Sunday Eucharist service. The four hymns that had been selected were all from 'Mission Praise' so this meant that they should be familiar to the congregation and there would be no need for Jennie to search for alternative hymn tunes. She immediately recognised the numbers of the first three hymns on the list: 251- How Sweet the Name of Jesus

Sounds; 327 - Immortal, Invisible and 142 - Jesus we love You. She didn't recognise hymn number 665, so she opened the hymnal to find out. It was 'The Spirit of the Lord' and she could see at a glance that it was not known either to herself or to the parishioners.

Jennie played it through, making quite a few mistakes as she did so, and she felt that the upbeat chorus would be too tricky for the congregation to manage, at least not without an in depth rehearsal session. She practiced it about six or seven times using the stopped diapason and the salicional organ stops for the verses, and added the melodic bourdon, open diapason and the gemshorn for the chorus. She then decided to have a quick run through of the other three hymns once more. Subsequently she played a few voluntaries, including Purcell's 'Gavotte' which was her all-time favourite. The first time that she had played the piece on this particular organ was at the end of a Eucharist Service about three or four years ago. It had been the first time that she had been asked to deputise for Pat Lewis and she had wanted to make a lasting impression. After the service, Ida Phillips had come up to the organ bench to tell Jennie that she felt as though she had been listening to a Cathedral instrument. Jennie had left the church that particular morning feeling even more uplifted than usual. She played hymn number 665 one more time before switching off the organ; she then locked the church door and returned to the vicarage.

As she was walking along the path she could see that a plastic carrier bag had been attached to the handle of her front door. Jennie thought that Mrs. Megan Beynon must have called by. Megan visited from time to time, bringing along a bara brith or a corned beef pie. Jennie accelerated her pace to find out what the good fairy had delivered this time. As she opened the bag on the kitchen table her eyes were met with the beautiful, golden pastry of a corned beef pie. She immediately cut a larger than average slice and sat down on the chair to eat it. She looked towards the kitchen clock which gave the time as a quarter to four. The day was far spent and she had very little to show for it. She was just about to put the carrier bag into her recycling bin, when she discovered a small piece of paper. It was a message from Megan, 'Eat and enjoy. Sorry I missed you. Only rang the bell once. Guess you're resting up. Luv, Megan xx.' Jennie would ring her later in the day to thank her for her generosity.

Jennie went to sit in the lounge. She put on the television to watch the afternoon film that was to begin at four o'clock. It was called 'Missing in Memphis' and the television guide had described it as a very moving portrayal of a young family's dilemma regarding their child's abduction. Jennie made herself comfortable on the sofa and watched the start of the programme, but even before the first commercial break appeared on the screen, she had fallen fast asleep. That is where Bryn found her when he arrived home at around six thirty that evening. She woke with a start in response to his voice. 'Lucky for some! Good film?'

She rubbed her eyes. She looked at the television screen to see Clint Eastwood standing outside a saloon. 'I don't know what this one is called. I fell asleep watching 'Missing in Memphis'.'

'Well, I'm glad that you have been able to relax. I'm zonked, if you'll pardon the expression. I think I'll sit down awhile to recharge my batteries and you can tell me how you've managed to fill your day.'

Jennie took a deep breath. 'Are you sitting comfortably?' she asked. 'Then I'll begin'.

She proceeded to give a short resume of the visit of Mrs. Lillian Shanks and the request for pear pies; the company of two men in boiler suits, and the three consecutive telephone calls regarding Sunday's service.

'By the way, who chose hymn number 665? You or Pat?'

'Pat must have,' replied Bryn. 'I told her 656 when she telephoned me to ask for the list of hymns', and he went on to sing the first verse of 'The Lord is King, lift up thy voice.'

'That certainly sounds more familiar than the one I was attempting to practice. I think that 665 in a 'no - no' for this parish.'

After a while Bryn stood up.

'Shall we go down to Yr Hen Efail for a meal, or are you too tired to bother?'

'I'm never too tired for Yr Hen Efail, Bryn,' she replied. 'It will be nice to just sit and relax together away from the door and the telephone. You can tell me all about your day.'

Bryn hurried upstairs in search of some 'civvies'. He intended to steer the conversation away from the day's agenda. There was absolutely no need for Jennie to know that Dai Trent had kept him waiting for a good twenty minutes. He'd overslept! She wouldn't really want to know that Bryn had been unanimously elected as chair of yet another committee. …And Bryn decided to keep the suggestions made in a little tete-a-tete with Bishop Anselm completely to himself for the time being. Jennie would find out soon enough as and when she was to become a host for a number of three week ordinand residential placements.

As he ran down the stairs he could see Jennie waiting by the open door. She was obviously ready for this. He caught hold of her hand and slammed the door behind him.

'Let's go,' he shouted and they ran down the vicarage path just like two adolescents running away from an ASBO!

CHAPTER 3: THE MOTHERS' UNION CHRISTMAS CONCERT.

JOY
HOLLY

One chilly and wet evening in mid October Bryn had received a series of telephone calls from Parishioners. He and Jennie had been sitting in the lounge watching the DVD of his nephew Matthew's wedding. During the summer Matthew had married Naomi, a childhood sweetheart, but the date of their marriage had coincided with Bryn and Jennie's holiday to Sorrento, so they were unable to be present. Bryn was inwardly pleased they were unable to attend the ceremony because it was to be held in Las Vegas, a place with which Bryn had no affinity whatsoever. Jennie, on the other hand, experienced a feeling of complete devastation and had even thought of asking Bryn about the possibility of changing their holiday plans. It was not only the wedding that excited her - that would be a brief and nippy affair, over in no time at all - it was the idea of walking down 'The Strip' and having a little flutter on the gaming machines that appealed to her more. To think that an ambition of a lifetime had almost been within her grasp! She would have been able to see at first hand 'Circus Circus' and 'The Golden Nugget.' She might even have brushed shoulders with a celebrity around the roulette table. There was even a chance of returning to Rhydbrychan with a fistful of dollars! The possibilities were endless.

The DVD had been delivered in the post about two weeks earlier, but this was the first occasion that Bryn and Jennie were spending an evening together since it had arrived.

During the first fifteen minutes or so of watching the 'Ceremony and Reception Highlights', as the DVD was called, Bryn had got up to answer the telephone three times. This was followed by almost a half hour break before the telephone rang again on four consecutive occasions.

The earlier calls were made by May, Jan Bevan, and Mrs. Ida Phillips, and the later ones by Tom Matthews. Phil Pugh, Meirion and Mrs. Lillian Shanks. They all spoke with one voice as it were, albeit at different times. It appeared that Mrs. Margaret Jones had been admitted to hospital with a suspected heart attack. Bryn had contacted the hospital after receiving the first telephone call, but he had been asked to call again a little later when he would be given more information. It appeared that Margaret was to be kept in hospital overnight at least, but Bryn was assured that an anointing and blessing was not necessary at this stage. It transpired that Margaret had not suffered a heart attack at all; apparently it was just a dreadful bout of indigestion.

Bryn was able to share this information with his flock as part of his announcements the following morning.

'I would like to stress how important it is that we, as clergy, are informed of such happenings. We rely on you completely for this sort of information. You are the town criers so to speak. As you are probably aware, neither Father Jeffrey nor I have crystal balls!' He picked up the weekly notice sheet. 'I would like to draw your attention to Tuesday's meeting in the vicarage at 7:00 p.m. Mrs. Beryl Francis has agreed that the Mothers' Union will be responsible for arranging our Christmas Entertainment this year.' Beryl had offered the services of the Branch, partly in jest, when she had been sitting alongside Bryn at a Coffee Morning in aid of Overseas earlier in the year and, until comparatively recently, she had completely forgotten about it. It was only when Bryn began to make enquiries that she remembered making the suggestion, and she didn't want to go back on her word.

'If there is anyone else who would like to participate, please come along to assist the members with their programme. We look forward to a good meeting. Thank you.' He then continued with the service.

For the past three years the Christmas entertainment had been a first class pantomime, performed by the Parish Players. All the church societies and groups had been involved in one way or another, either on stage, behind the scenes, with publicity or 'on the door'. Hitherto, the Mothers' Union had been 'on the door' or manning the shop during the interval. Although Jennie herself was a performer she could not envisage the members generally being able to provide a complete evening of entertainment.

The need for a completely different approach to this year's presentation was due to the fact that Father Edward Morgan had been called from the parish of St. Mary Magdalene to pastures new. He had been inducted as Curer of Souls at St. Peter's Derwen Fawr by Bishop Anselm early in the spring. Two coaches owned by Christiensen & Sons had transported over a hundred people to the service, and at least forty parishioners had travelled independently. He was, indeed, a very popular priest and had had a very successful ministry in Rhydbrychan. He had been caring to the community and devout in his devotions; he had been loved by the children and much loved by eligible females. The fact that he was ready and willing to dress in drag and prance about on the church hall stage was an added bonus!

Father Edward had assumed the responsibility of both producer and director of the pantomimes in addition to taking on the role of the Dame, which he performed most convincingly. The first two pantomimes, 'Sleeping Beauty' and 'Jack and the Beanstalk' ran for three nights only, from Thursday until Saturday, but the previous year's production of 'Aladdin' had been performed nightly for a whole week. All members of the cast felt the adrenalin going long after the final curtain call. Father Edward portrayed a magnificent Dame Dim-wit and Jennie had felt almost privileged to play the part of Whossit 'her' stooge. They had both enjoyed rehearsing their lines, practising their duets and working together on their dance routines. She wondered where the talent would lie for this year's effort. Was there a glimmer of a chance that Phyllis Rees, with her deep alto voice, could perform in drag a successful Frank Sinatra tribute? Jennie would have to wait and see what transpired at the Entertainment Meeting.

The time of Tuesday's meeting soon arrived and at five minutes to seven the doorbell rang. '*Do come in!*,' called Jennie as she walked towards the door. 'It's open.' The first to enter was Mrs. Lillian Shanks, followed closely behind by May and her daughter Helen.

'Come into the sitting room,' said Jennie pleasantly. 'Have a seat.'

Shortly afterwards the doorbell rang again, but since the door had been left ajar Beryl Francis, Jan Bevan and Pat Lewis took the initiative and walked straight in.

'We're in here,' said Jennie pointing in the direction of the sitting room. 'There are plenty of seats, so please go and sit down. Make yourselves at home.'

Mrs. Lillian Shanks welcomed them with an 'evening all' in a tone comparable to that of a television character of yesteryear. As someone was knocking on the glass pane of the door Jennie called, yet again, *'Do come in!'* She was in two minds as to whether she would quickly write out the words '*do come in*' on a piece of paper and stick it with blu-tack on the front door. She soon realised that this would not be necessary; a noble army of members were making their way in, so Jennie thought it unlikely that anyone else would be coming along.

'Hi Jennie', said Hilda Grey. 'I managed to *squeeze* seven of us into my people carrier.'

Jennie understood immediately the implication of the word 'squeeze'. Chris Pugh was among the passengers. She had confided in Jennie only the day before that she had topped the seventeen stone and that her doctor had given her some weight loss literature to read and was arranging for her to have an appointment with the dietician. Jennie was just about to close the door when she saw a hand reaching for the bell.

'No need, the door is open.' It was Martha Cwmdu. '*Do come in*, Martha.'

'I hope I'm not late. I had to wait for John to get back from the market. More sheep.'

As Jennie was about to close the door for a second time she heard a familiar voice call out her name. Lucy Richards had kindly given a lift to Miss Miriam Evans, Mrs. Ida Phillips and Mrs. Mabel Gwynne.

'Am I glad to see you Lucy,' said Jennie from the heart.

Here was talent at its best, a confident performer and an enthusiastic all rounder. Everybody liked Lucy and appreciated all that she did for the parish and beyond. She helped Jennie to carry some extra chairs into the sitting room but chose to sit on the floor herself, just incase there would be a late comer. In fact the chair remained vacant all evening as nobody else arrived. Jennie opened the meeting with some prayers from the Mothers' Union service book, then all members said the Mothers' Union Prayer together, followed by the Lord's Prayer. Jennie thanked everyone for coming and went on to ask if there were any apologies.

'I've received an apology from Mrs. Margaret Jones,' said Jennie. 'She says that she is feeling very much better and would like to thank everyone for their concern. She will be with us at the next meeting. Are there any other apologies?'

'Lynwen Porter can't get a babysitter,' said Pat, 'but count her in for whatever's happening. But she doesn't want to do anything on her own, she only wants to take part in the group items.'

'Apologies from Non Beavis. No reason given,' said Mrs. Lillian Shanks.

'Megan Beynon,' said Susan Walters. 'She had a bad experience with the chiropodist today. She said that it felt as though he had taken the sole off her foot along with the callous.'

'*Ahhhh! Sore!!!!*' exclaimed Thelma as a means of empathy… or otherwise!

Jennie chose to ignore the remark and went on to outline what she considered to be a possible programme. Maybe those present could become the Christmas Choir and provide a few choral items, particularly at the beginning and end of the concert. She also suggested that perhaps some instrumental items could be included and maybe some readings or poems. There was a wealth of seasonal subject matter available.

'Dafydd and I can sing a duet if you like,' said Susan Walters. 'We've been doing a bit of karaoke on the cruises. In fact we came third when we sang on 'The Ocean Wave' in the summer. We sang 'Some Enchanted Evening. Would that be any good?'

'It sounds splendid Sue, but we are trying to focus on seasonal items,' replied Jennie. 'Do you think you can manage a Christmas song instead?'

'Sure. We'll sort something out.'

Ida Phillips stood up to speak. 'I don't know if you are aware of the fact that I was a Blue Ribbon winner at the National Eisteddfod in the sixties. In fact, I have won countless solo competitions over the years and I will provide a solo for our Mothers' Union Christmas Concert this year.' Mrs. Ida Phillips meant business. She continued, 'I will give a rendering of 'Oh, Holy Night,' and I have the sheet music right here for Pat to practise.' She immediately handed the music to Pat, almost stumbling over Lucy, in her excitement to clinch the opportunity.

'An excellent choice Ida, but perhaps we could sing that as a choir piece. In fact it would be a very meaningful way to start off the concert. It would make a good introduction.' She paused for a moment, then continued, 'However, would you like to sing a few bars as a solo, 'a ray of hope, this weary world rejoices, for yonder breaks a new and glorious morn'.... for example?'

'That really isn't much of a solo Jennie. I don't normally sing a few bars; it's usually a complete piece. What if I continue with 'fall on your knees etc,' and the choir kneels down as I sing it? It would bring a bit of action into it….and it would be a prayerful approach with everyone knelt in quiet meditation. Then everybody could stand up for the last 'Oh night divine !' at the end of the aria.'

'It sounds as though you want us to be chorus girls, Mrs. Phillips and I'm not being one of *them*, thank you very much,' said Thelma. 'I've got too much cellulite for that.'

Phyllis looked very perturbed, 'Will the Vicar be standing in the wings Jennie? I think I might need a bit of help getting up. I'm waiting for a hip replacement.'

At the moment Jennie was keeping her thoughts to herself.

'Once I'm down, I'm down,' laughed Chris Pugh. 'It will take every member of the Men's Society to get me up again. I know what you mean, Phyllis.'

'One thing for sure, I won't be able to move quickly either, and unless we all kneel down and stand up at the same time we will make complete and utter fools of ourselves.' Miriam Evans knew what she was talking about. She had been the head-teacher of the church school until retiring a few years earlier. She had always insisted that the members of the school choir always stood up and sat down at the same time. She believed that it added a little professionalism to the performance.

Lillian Shanks spoke up. 'At this rate nothing is going to be decided. We are wasting time. If we require the assistance of an able bodied member of the clergy, equally able bodied members of the Men's Society, possibly along with volunteers of St. John's Ambulance and the Red Cross, all at the ready whilst we perform, then we are moving in the wrong direction. Moreover, to have such a crowd hiding back stage in order to pick up those who fall, would never comply with the present health and safety regulations. I think that the whole idea is ludicrous if you don't mind my saying so.'

A complete silence fell on the meeting. It was soon broken by Jennie.

'You said that you would be willing to sing 'O Holy Night' as a solo, Ida?'

'I would be delighted,' was the reply.

At last the programme was beginning to take shape.

'The choir items can be decided upon later. Let's press on,' said Jennie, 'but what about an instrumental contribution?'

'That's you Pat,' said Thelma. 'How about Dinah! Dinah! show us your leg?'

She stood up, lifted her skirt and did a couple of kicks in the air to endorse her suggestion. Jennie couldn't understand why Thelma always found the need to be coarse.

'Completely out of order,' said Lillian Shanks. 'The choice of lyric I mean, as opposed to an instrumental item itself. And what's more, it's hardly seasonal.'

Pat sensed that people were beginning to feel a little uncomfortable.

'Would you like me to play 'White Christmas?' she asked pleasantly. 'I'll bring the keyboard. It sounds beautiful when it's played on the strings.'

'Thank you Pat. That's a good idea. We're really getting somewhere now. We have choir items, a solo, a duet and an instrumental item. I hope that we will have a few more contributions though. Does anyone know the poem 'The night before Christmas'? That always goes down well. People always like to listen to a Christmas poem. I'm prepared to read John Betjeman's 'Christmas' if we're short of items.'

'I've never heard of John whatever you said, but I have written a few Christmas poems myself,' said Dwynwen Morris. Jennie was surprised to hear this because, as far as she was aware, Dwynwen had never participated as an individual before. She was always ready to do things as part of a group, whether it be preparing refreshments at Confirmations, or serving teas at functions or even cleaning the church. Jennie felt that she was about to see the real Dwynwen. She could barely conceal her excitement.

'This sounds really promising Dwynwen. Can you recite your poem 'off pat'?'

'It's got nothing to do with Pat. I made it up all by myself.' Dwynwen wasn't the brightest being on the block, by any stretch of the imagination. There was a lengthy ten second pause before Dwynwen began:

'Christmas in Bethlehem, by Dwynwen Morris,' she said quietly, and then she continued.

'It's Christmas,

Shhhhhhhhhhhhhhhhhhh!!!!!

Come to the stable

Shhhhhhhhhhhhhhhhhhh!!!!

Peep inside

Shhhhhhhhhhhhhhhhhhh!!!!

What do you see?

Shhhhhhhhhhhhhhhhhh!!!!

Quite a long silence prevailed. Eventually Jennie asked that 'Christmas in Bethlehem' by Dwynwen Morris be continued.'

'There's no more; that's it. I didn't want to make it too long incase people would get bored. All my poems are short. Would you like to hear another one? It's called 'Pudding' and she began reciting before Jennie could reply.

'I've a terrible pain in my tummy

Since eating my Christmas pud,

I think that I swallowed a pound coin,

Whatever, it's done me no good!'

'Thank you very much indeed Dwynwen. We really have something to work on here.'

Jennie looked across to Beryl Francis and wondered why on earth Beryl had suggested that the Mothers' Union be responsible for such an important event as the Christmas Concert. The whole community was expected to come along and support it. They always did. So far the meeting had been pretty disastrous. In fact it beggared belief what these ladies were coming up with. Surely Beryl realised that, although Jennie was a qualified teacher in performing arts, it was impossible for her to work with inane material. At present she could see no hope.

'I'll prepare the coffees now, but do continue with discussions. Is there anyone who would prefer tea?'

It was only Lillian Shanks who availed herself to the offered alternative. Lucy followed Jennie into the kitchen to give some help. They said nothing, but simply looked at each other in despair. Jennie wished that Bryn was home to express his opinion on the ideas that had been put forward or at least to give her a tad of moral support. How she wished that she had secretly video recorded this evening's get together so that it could be shown at a Diocesan Conference. It would leave The Dean and Chapter rolling in the aisles. But Jennie knew that this was serious business. A programme had to be arranged and arranged quickly at that, and she was overall responsible for what was to take place. As she and Lucy served the coffees and one tea, along with the bara brith and welshcakes, she was hoping that more achievable suggestions would be made.

'We'll continue with the meeting as we partake of the refreshments if that's alright,' said Jennie. 'Now, we're still open to offers for our entertainment.'

'I used to be able to walk twenty five yards balancing six books on my head. Now *that's* entertainment for you,' said Eiriannon Williams. 'I know it was a long time ago, over forty years in fact, but I'm willing to try again. All it needs is a bit of practice.'

'Our contributions have to be seasonal I'm afraid, Eiry,' emphasized Jennie.

'Yes, I know that,' Eiriannon replied. 'But I thought I might use Dicken's 'Christmas Carol' and a book of Christmas recipes amongst others. I think I can get my hands on a copy of 'A Child's Christmas in Wales' as well so I'm half way there already.'

For a moment nobody said anything, so Jennie thought that all the contributions, for what they were worth, had been made, but suddenly Chris Pugh began to speak.

'I have a *wonderful* idea. Very original!' she said. Everyone looked at her expectantly. 'You know those individual Christmas puddings? Well, I know that it would be against doctor's orders, bur I'm willing to try and see how many I could eat on stage in ten or fifteen minutes. On second thoughts, fifteen minutes might be stretching it, so let's say ten. That would encourage some audience participation as well, as they become involved in the proceedings with cheers and applause; well hopefully! I don't mind buying the puddings myself....so long as I can eat them myself. *Ha! Ha! Ha!* The idea just came to me out of the blue. What do you think Jennie?'

'I think that we have had some remarkable contributions offered here this evening and it certainly gives us food for thought.'

A bad choice of word she thought as soon as she had said it. She looked at Chris and smiled. 'Thank you for your enthusiasm.' Jennie took a short breather to regain her composure. Although she was beginning to feel somewhat frail and feeble she tried to remain positive. 'I'm sure that we can combine as a Christmas Choir with some solo items and readings,' she said amiably, 'but we cannot possibly draw up a programme tonight. I will put your many and varied suggestions to the vicar and we'll take it from there. Thank you all so very much for your contributions.'

After the ladies had all left Jennie cleared away. She was glad to have some 'time out.' She didn't like the expression, but she had to admit that this meeting had been '*the pits*'. There was absolutely no other way to describe it. She decided that putting on a Christmas concert with special needs children, along with all the histrionics and hysteria that went with it, was a much easier and far more manageable alternative.

Lucy had offered to stay behind to help to clear up but, knowing that she had transported some of the more elderly ladies to the meeting, Jennie thought it best that she took them home directly. As she was putting the remaining welshcakes into the cake tin she wondered how many of these Chris Pugh could consume in a given length of time. Since they were of less weight, smaller and more easily digestible than the individual Christmas puddings; maybe she could advance on two dozen!

When everything was back to normal, Jennie went into the lounge to sit down. She felt absolutely exhausted. She had not chaired a meeting such as this in all her years as Branch Leader and the experience had left her feeling devastated and traumatised.

When she looked at the clock she could see that the time was 9:30 p.m. Jennie attempted a flash-back on the meeting. It was true to say that very little had been accomplished during the two or more hours that the members had been there. She had been very impressed with the number of ladies that had turned up, but it was quality and not quantity that she was looking for and, although there had been a number of contributions offered, she regarded most as being inappropriate or unsuitable.

Those who were willing to perform solos, she believed, had passed their sell-by date, and the work of their Poet Laureate lacked depth and emotion. Over seventies could hardly be expected to give a 'knees bend! arms stretch!' in synchrony, and a member of the Mothers' Union walking across the stage balancing six seasonal books on her head could hardly be regarded as Christmas entertainment. For someone to be gorging Christmas puddings for a ten minute duration was completely obscene, especially when there was so much hunger and genuine need in the world.

It was a case of back to the drawing board. So far there were only a couple of items that seemed to be of quality. She was dubious, to say the least, of the standard of achievement aboard 'The Ocean Wave' regarding karaoke competitions. Perhaps she could arrange a meeting with Bryn, Beryl Francis and Lucy and see what they could come up with between them. The fewer the number of people, the greater the chances of a successful outcome. Such was her dictum as she turned out the light in the lounge and made her way upstairs. Just as she was getting into bed, she heard Bryn coming in. He had been to a meeting regarding the reorganisation of parishes.

'I'm up here,' called Jennie.

'I'm coming up now,' Bryn responded as he hurried up the stairs. 'What a meeting!' he exclaimed as he walked into the bedroom. 'I could hardly believe my ears at some of the things that were being said, and from people you thought would know better. The only good thing about it was the light buffet.'

Whilst he was speaking he undressed and put on his pyjamas.

'Do you know that somebody even suggested that we held a Quiet Day in order to pray about the amalgamation of the parishes, then there was the old faithful suggestion of a working party being set up.'

He went into the spare bedroom to hang up his cassock. 'A follow-up meeting is to be held in January, but no date was decided,' he continued. 'Dai Trent was most unpleasant and referred to the hierarchy of the diocese as being nothing more than a puff of wind. Bishop Anselm had really lost it by the end. He asked us all to stand for the National Anthem, but quickly corrected himself and led us in saying the Grace.' Bryn paused. 'That's more than enough from me. I'm sure that you had a much more pleasant evening and I trust that the Mothers' Union Christmas Concert is signed, sealed and delivered as it were.'

'Come to bed, love. Can we forget about the concerts and parishes, bishops, priests and deacons and focus on a good night's rest. We can continue this discussion in the morning. Goodnight. Sleep tight and if the bugs bite keep it to yourself.'

'Can't you adapt one of the Christmas plays that you wrote for the children in school?' enquired Bryn the following morning, having received a blow by blow account of Jennie's catastrophic evening. He was only trying to be helpful. 'You must be joking,' answered Jennie. 'Maybe Phyllis Rees would make a decent 'Artaban,' but what would I do for the other three wise men from the east? She's the only member of the group whose voice I could work on. As for 'Baboushka' I would be spoilt for choice - so many grannies - and if I were to consider presenting 'Christmas Around the World', the characters would have to be prepared to dress up as cowboys and indians; we'd need a Saint Lucy who'd be willing to wear a wreath with lighted candles on her head and a few really good sports to wear lederhosen. Knowing my luck at the moment, the only volunteer for lederhosen would be Chris Pugh. Quite honestly, Bryn, I don't think it would work. Do you?'

'Maybe not. It was just a thought.'

Bryn decided that, as Jennie had suggested, they would hold an informal meeting with Mrs. Beryl Francis and Lucy as soon as possible. Fortunately they were all free on Thursday evening and, if something specific could be arranged there and then, rehearsals could begin straight away.

By some means Mrs. Jean Powell, who was the present head-teacher of the St. Mary Magdalene Voluntary Aided School, had heard about Tuesday's meeting and had telephoned the vicarage the following morning to offer some participation by the children, if it was required.

As soon as Mrs. Beryl Francis walked through the vicarage door she apologised profusely for even suggesting that the Mothers' Union take on such a feat and, although she had been half joking at the time, she had thought that it would make a nice change for them - meaning that they could be away from the door and the kitchen of the church hall, and have the opportunity to try out something completely different. Mothers' Union members were known for their domestic skills but Beryl wanted them to display some of their other talents. 'I'm sure that the choir items will be successful,' she said.

Jennie agreed and went on to say, 'We may even be able to sing a few of the more familiar carols in two parts, or even with descant as well. It was mainly the suggestions offered by individuals that left me speechless.'

'I'll help in any way that I can,' said Lucy. 'I didn't speak up in the meeting, because I was really embarrassed by what was going on. I couldn't believe my ears at some of the ideas, but everyone seemed to be so serious about what they were willing to do.'

However, that very evening, within the four walls of the vicarage the small group managed to compile a tentative programme, including a number of items to be performed by the Christmas Choir. That meant that practices could soon be in full swing.

Lucy volunteered to sing a couple of solos and also suggested that her Sunday School class might like to sing 'Santa Claus is coming to Town' and 'Rudolph the Red Nosed Reindeer'. It was at this point that the original title for the evening, 'Carolling by Candlelight' was changed to 'Christmas by Candlelight' so that they could get away with using more secular items in the programme. Pat would play two instrumentals on her keyboard and Mrs. Margaret Jones, who had now fully recovered from her flatulence, would recite T S. Elliott's 'Journey of the Magi'. She had been a teacher of elocution and dance and could always be relied upon to give a polished performance. It seemed that with all this, along with Ida Phillips's solo and the proposed duets by Susan and Dafydd Watkins, things were very much in hand. Jennie was feeling better, not so much by the minute but by the decision of each item. Things were moving forward at break-neck speed….well…. in comparison to Tuesday's meeting!

Jennie would approach Mrs. Jean Powell regarding a few contributions by the school children to round off the evening. Many of the pupils attended Sunday School, so Bryn thought that it was right and proper for them to be involved.

Jennie was delighted at the outcome of this meeting. If truth be known, she had had a couple of sleepless nights and restless days as her thoughts and mind mulled over all sorts of possible Christmas entertainment. At one point, in sheer desperation, she had considered contacting Merlin the Magician and paying him out of her own pocket. If it hadn't have been four o'clock in the morning when she was considering this she probably would have done so. She felt confident that, from here-on in, everything would go smoothly.

The Mothers' Union Christmas Concert, or 'Christmas by Candlelight' as it was now called, was held in St. Mary Magdalene Church Hall on the Wednesday before Christmas. The building was full to capacity and even Elvis

Presley would have found it difficult to leave the building! Every ticket had been sold and many people paid at the door, but this domain was under the jurisdiction of the church treasurer Mr. Tom Matthews, assisted by Father Jeffrey. The Men's Society was in charge of the mince pies and mulled wine, and the churchwardens were overseeing the tea-lights and candles, to make sure that they did not become a health and safety issue, and the only people allowed back-stage were those who were actually taking part.

The evening's entertainment was a resounding success. The Mothers' Union Choir began the performance with 'Mary's Boy Child', sung in two part harmony. They all looked very elegant in their long red skirts green tops and black velvet jackets. Their second item was a delightful rendering of 'Look to the Skies' followed by 'The Holly and the Ivy', during which Ida Phillips, Phyllis Rees and Jennie each sang a solo verse. Pat was the next performer on the programme; she played 'White Christmas' on the keyboard as arranged. When she had finished the melody, Bryn asked if she would play it through again, so that those who wished to could sing along to this all time favourite. Bryn gave the microphone to Phyllis so that she could lead the singing.

As soon as she started Jennie recognised the potential of performing a creditable Bing Crosby/Frank Sinatra tribute anywhere, anytime. Margaret Jones was next, and she recited T. S. Elliot's 'The Journey of the Magi' as it had never been narrated before. She could have easily won an Oscar for that performance had one been available in Rhydbrychan at the time. She was an extremely gifted woman.

Dafydd and Susan had decided to sing 'Baby it's cold outside' as their duet for the first half of the programme. This was an ideal choice since the predicted temperature for the evening was sub zero. They both had beautiful voices and their facial expression and body talk enhanced their presentation. Like everybody else in the hall that evening, Jennie was very impressed with the couple. She had seen them practising a few times at rehearsals and they had been very good, but tonight they had been slick and stylish and had given a remarkable performance.

Next on the programme was Lucy; she sang two songs, one of which she had composed herself for a radio competition in which she was a runner up. It was called 'Little Jesus sweetly lay' in which she described the obedience of the Virgin Mary, the patience of Joseph and the joy of the shepherds and the angels. She sang it with such emotion that Mrs. Ida Phillips was close to tears. She then led her Sunday School class in 'Under Bethlehem's star so bright' and the audience became so carried away that they couldn't help but join in the '*hydom! hydom! tiddlydum!*' chorus.

The Mothers' Union Choir brought the first half of the programme to an end with a lively and amusing version of 'The Twelve Days of Christmas.' Phyllis Rees and Martha (Cwmdu) were positively gasping for breath by the end of the last verse, and Phyllis Rees said that she was willing to forego her hip replacement in preference to a heart transplant!

A twenty minute interval followed, during which time the mulled wine and mince pies were served. There was also a queue building up in front of a small booth at the back of the hall, where pop and crisps could be purchased. Charles Harris was proclaiming his 'buy one get one free!', but nobody believed him. Most people were used to his nonsense by now. When everybody had been catered for Father Jeffrey announced that it was time to draw the raffle.

'Good Evening ladies and gentlemen, boys and girls. We are all certainly having a feast of entertainment this evening and there's more to come. So now we'll do the raffle. Do you all have your tickets ready? We have three prizes, so there will be three lucky winners. The first prize is a voucher for £25, the second prize is a £20 voucher and the third prize is one for £10...all for the same store but it's not just *any* store! O.K. then. Good luck everybody! We are using *Genevieve* tonight by the way,' and he stared to roll the barrel.

The lucky winners were Dwynwen Morris, Ken Thomas and Nobby Belcher from Lwff-y-dwlb. He had bought the ticket from Jennie the day before, when he had called in at the vicarage to deliver a Christmas card.

The children from the school opened the second half of the programme with 'Away in a Manger'. Little Sophie Walters was dressed as Mary and her older brother Stephen proved to be a very caring Joseph, especially when, during the second verse Mary began to swing the newborn Baby Jesus above her head. 'Give him here!' he was heard to say, and being ever obedient she did so. Joseph jumped at the opportunity to display his paternal qualities, even to the point of attempting to check the baby's napkin.

Mrs. Ida Phillips then came on stage, taking a few pre-performance bows as she made her way to the microphone. When everybody was quiet she nodded at Pat, indicating that she was ready to begin her magnum opus. She gave a true Blue Ribbon performance right up until the final cadence when she endeavoured to reach top 'A' instead of settling for the 'F' as she had done in the rehearsals.

Consequently the night, though still Holy, was not quite as divine as it might have been! Even so, she left the stage to rapturous applause.

Lucy and her class performed another two items, one being 'The Night before Christmas,' which was an excellent example of choral speaking. The other item was 'The Shepherds Rap' which the children had made up themselves during a recent Sunday School lesson. It was absolutely hilarious, with the shepherds falling over their snow white *sheep* as they stumbled down the mountain *steep* and they pushed and they shoved, shouting *beep! beep! beep!*! to get a glimpse of the baby fast *asleep*!!. The performers received a standing ovation. This would be a hard act to follow, but in a sense, the way had been paved for Sue and Dafydd's 'Have yourself a merry little Christmas' which they sang like real professionals. This was followed by a group of Key Stage 1 pupils reciting a very amusing poem based on the theme 'My Gran wants an Action Man and I'll get her one if I can!' The poem went on to explain that after a few hiccups an action man was found, so Gran could expect company for Christmas. She may be past believing in Santa Claus but she was obviously ready for a bit of action over the festive period!

The programme was brought to an end with two items by the Mothers' Union Choir. Firstly they sang 'Three Kings from Persian Lands Afar' which was followed by 'The Bells Ring Out at Christmastime'. They were joined on stage by all the other performers to sing 'We Wish You A Merry Christmas.' Chris Pugh was quite beside herself as she performed the actions indicating that they all loved figgie pudding and they had no intention of leaving until they had some. Bryn was very tempted to throw her the one that Gaynor had secretly placed under his chair during the interval, but decided against it! After all, charity begins at home and Gaynor's Christmas puddings were second to none!

Jennie was very impressed with the quality of performance by all the participants. She knew that Lucy was an extremely talented young lady, and that whatever she chose to present would be enjoyed and appreciated by everyone, but she hadn't expected others to reach such a high standard. The fact that the evening had gone so smoothly and successfully was unbelievable. The members of the Mothers' Union had become artistes in their own right and Jennie was very proud of their achievements. It just went to show what could be done when people worked together for the common good. Everybody had enjoyed a wonderful evening together.

Bryn brought the proceedings to a close by thanking everyone who had helped to make the evening such a success. It had been a very pleasant evening indeed and he asked the audience to show their appreciation once more. He reminded the children about the Crib Service on Christmas Eve and told the grans to get as much action as possible out of those men because such men were not always easy to come by. He explained that to have a man of action in the comfort of one's home over the Christmas Season, was certainly worth two in the bush for the rest of the whole year. To this he received unexpected and unprecedented applause. He then gave a Seasonal Blessing and wished everyone present, along with their loved ones wherever they may be, a very happy and a blessed Christmastide.

A good number of people remained behind to stack the chairs and help where they could, in order to restore the hall to its former glory, as it were. Although Non Beavis, the church cleaner, had asked Bryn to leave it all for her to deal with the next day, he decided on this occasion, although on this occasion only, to disregard her request. By the time everyone had completed their tasks, all that was left for Non to do the following day was to check the toilets and empty the bins. Bryn considered this to be enough of a chore for any member of the human race, especially after an enormous soiree such as this.

'Would you and Jen like to join some of us in 'Yr Hen Efail' for a nightcap, Bryn?' asked Meirion.

Bryn walked towards the stage where Jennie was standing. She was congratulating Sue and Dafydd on their outstanding performance. He asked her if she wanted to join some of the parishioners for a beverage, as he put it.

'We might as well,' she replied. 'The adrenalin is still on a high, so it would be nice to relax in convivial company. What about you?'

'Why not? Christmas comes but once a year.'

'And when it comes it brings good cheer,' they said in unison as they walked through the church hall doors. Huw Martin had volunteered to have a final check through the building and lock up before he went to join the others.

When Bryn looked at his watch later, he was amazed to see that it was well past mid-night. He wasn't sure if 'Yr Hen Efail' had been granted extended licensing hours, but that was of no concern to him, so he made a final trip to the bar to purchase drinks for all those members of his flock who were still in situ. There were four gin and tonics, three pints on the first tray that he carried and two whiskies, a vodka and tonic and a coke and a glass of port for himself on the second. 'Happy Christmas everyone,' he said as he sat down. By the time that he and Jennie were snug in their bed, it was going on for two o' clock in the morning. Neither of them were used to keeping such late hours so they went to sleep immediately. Both of them had been quite overcome by the evening's proceedings; the parishioners of St. Mary Magdalene, Rhydbrychan had excelled themselves yet again and had provided the community with a very meaningful start to the Christmas celebrations.

Part 2:
2002

Chapter 4: WORKMEN AND SCAFFOLDING

The weather during early November 2001 had been very wet and windy. The village had endured gale force winds and a much heavier than average rainfall. There had even been a red flood alert for those residences within close proximity of the River Maldwyn, so the occupants of Heol-y-Beirdd, Rhydbrychan had been issued with sandbags as a precaution. Fortunately, despite the increasingly heavy rainfalls, no damage had been caused to their properties. The weather forecast predicted a mild spell for the next few weeks, but there was more rain to come.

It was at about this time that Jennie noticed a leak in the ceiling of the back bedroom, which was recognised in the vicarage as being the guest bedroom. Drips of water seemed to be falling intermittently on to the wooden flooring at the foot of the bed. She had placed a blue plastic bucket with matching blue bowl as strategically as possible below the leaks, and had been emptying them as and when necessary, just as one would empty a chamber pot in the good old days. Bryn had duly informed Brian Smith, the Property Manager, who assured him that he would come and view the problem within the next fortnight although Brian had stated emphatically that he was a very busy man at present, due to the fact that many of the properties owned by the Parsonage Board had reported problems of one sort or another as a result of the adverse weather conditions. He assured Bryn that he would visit St. Mary Magdalene Vicarage in mid-

December. It would definitely be before Christmas and he felt confident that, from Bryn's description of the problem, things could be quickly rectified. Unfortunately, due to an unexpectedly heavy snowfall, the December appointment was cancelled and, for some reason or another, no further arrangements had been made.

Betty, Jennie's mother, always used the guest room when she came to stay but Jennie wasn't going to put anything to chance, although Bryn assured her that nothing major was likely to happen.

'Your mother likes that room,' Bryn had said. 'You can empty the bowls before she gets up in the morning and before she goes to bed at night then she won't know a thing.'

When she arrived for her Christmas / New Year break Betty was offered a choice of sleeping accommodation. She expressed the fact that she didn't want to be in the firing line of a masonry shoot-out or an unforeseen downpour, so she chose the small bedroom to the front - the one without the en-suite! She realised that squeezing past the old wooden box and several other large, bulky items that were stored there, would be a challenge to be reckoned with, but her motto was 'better to be safe than sorry.' As it happened, her visit was very pleasant and completely uneventful and Betty experienced one of her best Christmases ever. This was partly due to the fact that she had her daughter's complete attention since there was no need for Jennie to excuse herself to see to lesson preparation or read through educational documentation.

However, it wasn't until the first week of February that Bryn noticed that the problem in the guest room had worsened dramatically. He had gone in to fetch his biretta from the drawer in the dressing table; although he hadn't worn it for some time, he thought that since the parish was celebrating the Festival of Candlemas he would wear his biretta to church and his skull cap during the service. He felt that such liturgical accessories would be acceptable on this feast day, particularly as he had arranged for Father Jeffrey to fill the thurible with incense for the occasion. As he walked into the guest room, he noticed immediately that part of the ceiling had actually caved in and there was debris on the bed, on the windowsill, on the bedside cabinet and on the floor. The room was a disaster zone!

'Jennie!' he called plaintively. 'Jennie, come quickly! We have a problem….a mega problem at that.'

Bryn wasn't usually subject to histrionics, so she was conscious of the fact that things were not right; she had checked the room the previous day, and had emptied half a bowlful of water, so something alarming must have happened during the past twenty four hours. She responded to the call at the same pace as the emergency services are expected to respond to a 999 call so, as she ran up the stairs, she sang '*na! na! na! na!*' attempting to bring a little humour to the situation. When she arrived at the guest room, she could see Bryn standing to the right of the bed, which was covered in debris, and the matching blue bucket and bowl had been filled almost to capacity. So much had happened in a short space of time. Everything had been as well as could be expected when she had inspected the room the day before. They stood in silence, not even daring to make eye contact, knowing in their heart of hearts that the site was in desperate need of workmen. They had experienced the company of workmen in each of their parsonage properties and for the most part, had found them lethargic and languid and their work schedule invariably exceeded the proposed date of completion.

'Look on the bright side,' said Jennie. 'At least there were no guests using the room at the time. Just think, your very own mother-in-law could have been sleeping there when the catastrophe occurred.'

Bryn said nothing in response; he just gave a cynical smirk.

'By the way,' said Jennie, trying to make light of the situation, 'Did I tell you that she would like to come over on St. David's Day for a few nights? She wants to come to the Cawl Supper in the church hall.'

'You hadn't mentioned anything, but it will be fine. She will have to sleep in the small front room though, like she did at Christmas. I can't see this room being sorted by then. On the other hand, one never knows one's luck!'

Bryn had some uncertainties about his mother-in-law and, although they did not always see eye to eye, they showed a unique respect for each another. They were both learned individuals. Bryn had grasped every opportunity that had come his way to further his knowledge; consequently he had continued his studies and had gained an M.Phil.

Betty, on the other hand, had been forced to leave school at an early age to care for a younger sibling, and although she was the top student in the scholarship examination as it was called in those days, it had not been possible for her to go on to any sort of further education. Even so, now at the age of ninety- five, although being almost completely self-taught, she had a wealth of general knowledge. Bryn had responded to his calling with excitement and dedication; Betty, however, had been unable to follow her 'dream' of becoming a librarian. Nevertheless, she had been an ardent reader over many years, and was more than capable of holding her own in all aspects of discussion, apart, perhaps, from facts and figures relating to the motoring industry! She regarded the fact that she was able to complete the crossword in the 'Church Times' before Bryn had even found a pen as a paramount achievement. All differences aside, she regarded Bryn as a devout priest, a man of knowledge and a devoted husband to her only daughter Jennie.

Brian Smith, Diocesan Properties Manager, finally arrived at St. Mary Magdalene Vicarage on March 2nd at 11:00 a.m. Neither Bryn nor Jennie were at home at the time, and neither had remembered to notify Betty of the arrangements. The doorbell rang at eleven o' clock precisely. Betty was making her way to the door when the bell rang for a second time.

'Just a minute, please; I know I'm slow,' she called in rather a hoarse voice.

When she finally got to the door, she found it difficult to open, due to arthritis in her hands.

'I'm doing my best. Shouldn't be long!'

With that the door opened with such force it almost sent Betty in a complete turn around.

'Hello! Can I help you?' she asked politely. 'I'm Jennie's mother.'

'Hello! I'm Brian Smith and I've come to view the property.'

'With all due respect, Mr. Smith, this property is not for sale. It is owned by the Church in Wales and it is occupied.'

'Yes, I know that Mrs...er...'

'Owen.'

'Mrs. Owen, I am the Property Manager for the Diocese. There seems to have been some problems with the ceiling of late and I have come to survey the scene.'

'I don't think that there is much ceiling for you to survey, Mr. Smith, but *do come in* and see for yourself. Do you intend going upstairs to view the damage independently or would you like me to try and clamber up behind you. If so, I'll need to get my walking stick from the kitchen.'

'I'll manage fine, thank you Mrs. Owen. I know the property well.'

Betty was just about to read the newspaper when Brian Smith suddenly appeared in the kitchen.

'I'm done, Mrs. Owen,' he said. 'It could well be a big job.'

'Goodness, gracious me that was quick!' she replied. 'Are you sure that you had a good look? To all intents and purposes, Mr. Smith, the place reminds me of the aftermath of an explosion. I hope that this doesn't mean that Jennie has to have an 'open house' for workmen again. Sufficient unto the day is the evil thereof! Biblical quote!'

Brian Smith explained to Betty that he would need to come back again. He would wear his boiler suit in order to be suitably dressed to investigate any possible problems in the attic. She noticed how well-dressed he was for somebody who should be ready to meet dirt, dust, grunge and grime as part of his daily work.

The fact that he was wearing a smart pin striped suit, a white shirt, a blue polka dot dickey bow and black patent shoes left Betty feeling most bewildered. It seemed so inappropriate. She thought that an equally extreme situation could be Bryn turning up to conduct a funeral dressed in his shortest shorts and his 'I am the Greatest!' T-shirt. It would cause the bereaved family to be more confused even than Betty was at this time.

Mr. Smith left the premises and drove down the drive at what appeared to Betty, nothing less than break - neck speed. She could see and hear that this model was far superior to Bryn's 'get-you-from-A-to-B-if-you're lucky' counterpart. Betty returned to the kitchen and began to read the newspaper. She always enjoyed her breaks at the vicarage and both Jennie and Bryn were always so very kind to her. Before too long Jennie came back from the Mothers' Union Eucharist.

'Were there any phone calls?' she asked as she entered the kitchen.

'No, but a Mr. Brian Smith has been here looking at the ceiling - or lack of it. What a smartly dressed man and a stylish car......I'm sure that he thought that he was the bee's knees with that machete.'

'I think you mean Mercedes, Mum.'

'Do I? Well, he's coming back in his boiler suit so that he can have a good look in the attic. He said that it could be a big job.'

'Did he say when he was coming back?'

'No, he only mentioned his boiler suit and the possibility of a big job.'

Jennie took the notepad from alongside the telephone and placed it on the table. Then she took a ballpoint pen from her handbag and breathed deeply. She sang 'Workmen and Scaffolding! Workmen and Scaffolding!' substituting the words of 'Meekness and Majesty' in Mission Praise, and continued to sing 'I will proceed with a twenty year review!'

She sat at the kitchen table to make a note of all the structural improvements that she had experienced in the various places where they had lived during Bryn's thirty years of ministry.

20 Park View (Curacy - The Parish of St. David's, Bro Celynnen)

- erection of scaffolding

- removal of chimney

- dismantling of scaffolding

- installation of oil central heating to replace storage heaters

- oil leak in kitchen one week after installation

- kitchen flooring completely replaced (as a result of oil leak)

St Catherine's Vicarage, Capel Deiniol (1st Incumbency)

- cesspit information with-held. It was a case of what the eye don't see......until taken over by another of the five senses!

- replacement of ancient and dangerous gas fire.

St. Teilo's Vicarage, Llanelfed (2nd Incumbency)

- erection of scaffolding

- five-yearly painting of exterior walls, window sills etc.

- extension to study (4 month duration)

-use of spare bedroom as makeshift study during this period

- dismantling of scaffolding

St. Michael and All Angels, Pont Gwallter, with St. Luke's Cwmcaredig (3rd Incumbency)

- unfinished work on arrival at vicarage

- the walls of three bedrooms had been painted a luminous purple in error

- unfinished flooring in utility room

- no toilet seat or washbasin in downstairs cloakroom

- ongoing work regarding the dampness in dining room, with workmen's paraphernalia scattered around to prove it

St. Mary Magdalene Vicarage, Rhydbrychan (present position)

- wasp's nest removed from attic location

- double-glazed windows installed as an alternative to the defective sash system

- new gas boiler fixed as a result of incessant 'call outs'

- dampness in sitting room alleviated

Jennie felt that she would like to share this information with her mother who was enjoying reading the morning newspaper.

'I can see that you are enjoying the politics section there, and I don't really want to disturb your morning update on what's happened in Westminster, but I have something to report.'

'What's that, Jennie?' asked Betty.

Jennie proceeded to read out the many and varied aspects of manual labour that she had experienced over the years.

'It's going to happen again, Mum,' she said. 'I'm going to have to meet more workmen.'

'Most of them are very nice I'm sure,' replied Betty, 'And look on the bright side; it will probably be just workmen….. no scaffolding, although we have to be realistic I suppose

Jennie; it seems that now we're in the twenty first century they customarily go hand in hand.'

About two weeks later, as Jennie was walking down the vicarage drive to go to the local shop to collect the current edition of the 'Church Times' a motor bike passed her as speedily as a railway train makes its inter-city journeys. She thought that the rider must have been taking part in some sort of rally and had, in his enthusiasm, taken the wrong route. She hurried back up the drive as quickly as she could to ensure that all was well.

'Excuse me!' she called as the rider removed his helmet. She recognised him at once, as Mr. Brian Smith.

'I know I'm almost an hour early, Jennie, but, I'm trying to buzz around as quickly as I can this morning. I've got a meeting this afternoon in Llanmaldwyn and I have to go to the Diocesan office, and I need to see the bishop before that, so I won't keep you long.' Jennie opened the door and they both walked into the kitchen.

'It's OK Jennie, don't panic,' said Brian as he began to remove his leathers. 'I've got my boiler suit on underneath all this regalia. There's no way that I'm going to perform the full monty here or anywhere else! Of course the new Archdeacon's wife seems to be a bit of a girl, so she might well appreciate a bit of horse play but I don't have time for that at the moment. Hope you don't mind! Anyway, I'm going up to the loft. It's a good thing that we had that ladder fixed last year. It's a great improvement to the rickety, old stepladder that we had depended on for so long and that had almost become a mutual friend.'

Jennie decided to empty the dishwasher so as not to waste any time. She had a busy day ahead; this included a Deanery Quiet Afternoon for Mothers' Union members and she had been asked to lead the intercessions towards the end of the service. However, before Jennie had even finished with the dishwasher, Brian appeared in the doorway of the kitchen.

'It's bad news, I'm afraid, Jennie. It looks as though we will have to replace the roofing. I know that several of my predecessors have, over time, made an effort to patch it up, but we can't go on like this anymore. It would be ridiculous even to attempt another make over.'

Jennie tried to conceal her feelings and smilingly she asked Brian, 'What will this mean for day to day living here in the vicarage?'

'*Workmen and Scaffolding!*' was the reply.

Brian assured Jennie that the scaffolding would be up by the end of the week and that the work would begin as soon as possible after that. He graciously declined her offer of a cup of coffee and, speaking inaudibly through his crash helmet, explained that he was on his way to the Bishop's Palace to arrange the installation of an impressive garden feature.

Brian Smith was true to his word and by the Saturday of that week the vicarage was completely surrounded by scaffolding and the workmen were due to start at 8:30 a.m. the following Monday. As no-one had shown up by 9:15 a.m. Jennie was beginning to wonder if she had miscalculated the date and time of the commencement of the work. By 9:45a.m., however, she could see from the sitting room window that a large truck had pulled up on the forecourt. She could see two men walking towards the side of the house. Jennie decided to go upstairs to the window on the landing from where she could take a closer look.

Three men were still sitting in the cab; one was reading a newspaper, another was pouring a drink from a thermos flask and the third was dragging at a cigarette. As she was making her way downstairs the door bell rang. It seemed to be more piercing than usual and its duration far exceeded that of the customary visitor. Jennie opened the door.

'Hya love! I'm Darren from Colin's Constructions. My mates are out by 'ere, but I need a can desperate love.'

Jennie went on to explain that she only kept diet drinks in the house, but that he was very welcome to one of those since he appeared to be so very agitated. It emerged that she was on a completely different wave length and that Darren really needed to use the toilet. During the coming weeks she couldn't help but notice that he seemed to divide his time equally between jobs! Two other men then called through the open door to introduce themselves.

'Yoo-hoo Missus!' Jennie walked towards the porch. 'Nice to meet you missus. I'm Gavin - you can call me Gav if you like and my mate by 'ere is Rick. I take milk and two sugars but 'e don't take no sugar, only milk.'

Jennie smiled at them politely, but said nothing. She walked towards the van; two of the workmen were out of the cab by now, but the third remained inside finishing his cigarette.

'More butts to enhance the premises,' she thought to herself.

'How-be Mrs. Jenkins! I'm Colin. Him by 'ere is Dave and him by there in the cab is Jonathan, but we call him Fag ash Fred 'cause we can't get him to kick the habit.'

'Would you like me to provide an ash tray? asked Jennie pleasantly.

'Too dangerous on the scaffolding Mrs. Jenkins. He could trip over it see. Best for him to stubb 'em out as and when. Come on, mate! Let's get started.'

He called again in the direction of the cab, 'Come on!! Let's get going,' and they all disappeared around the back of the house.

Shortly afterwards Jennie left to drive to Lwff -y- dwlb to collect her mother who was due to stay for a few days, and by the time they got back the premises were completely free of Colin's Constructions and all that it entailed. By 8:45 a.m. the following morning, however, the patter of plimsols could be heard on the scaffolding. Jennie felt as though she should warn the surrounding area...... BEWARE!!!.... MEN AT WORK!!!

Betty had almost completed the crossword in the daily newspaper when there was a tap on the kitchen window. It was Darren. He was making some unusual gestures and performed what appeared to Betty to be some sort of Highland Fling. She went to the window to try to hear what he had to say but, since the performance continued and she had no idea as to what was going on, she shouted 'Oh, do what you like!' and she returned to the kitchen table and to her crossword puzzle, quite oblivious to Darren's whereabouts.

Shortly afterwards a voice came from the vicinity of the downstairs cloakroom. 'Thanks Gran!' She was stunned at such familiarity.

As he made a detour to the scaffolding he passed by the kitchen window giving a loud rap and a thumbs up as he went. A little later on the doorbell rang.

'*Do come in!*,' called Betty from the kitchen.'The door *is* open.' In walked a very well built young man with his hair tied back in a long pony tail.

"Hya love! I'm Gav. Any chance of a cuppa? I'm parched.'

He smacked his lips together several times.

'You're asking *me* to make you *tea*?' questioned Betty poetically. 'I was under the impression that workmen always provided their own refreshments.'

'My missus went and dropped my flask just when she was filling it this morning. I got a few bottled waters but I feel like something hot. It's no joke working on a roof love, you want to be there!'

'I most certainly do *not* want to be there young man. I am over ninety years of age and I have no intention of negotiating scaffolding in order to get a bird's eye view of roof repairs. Would you please help yourself? The storage jars are clearly marked,' and she slowly walked away from it all into the sitting room, leaving Gavin to fend for himself.

One morning during the fourth week of roof renovation Jennie woke with a severe migraine. She called downstairs to Bryn, who was working in the study, and asked him to pass her the medication that she took at times like this, along with a glass of cold water. She knew that she would have to remain in bed and try to sleep it off; there was no other cure.

'You haven't had one of these for a very long time,' Bryn said as he gave her the tablets.

'Let's hope it will soon clear. I should be back by lunchtime. Deanery meetings don't usually take very long.' He paused. 'Although it might take a little longer today. We have to submit names for a new Area Dean. Dai Trent thinks he's in the running, though, if you ask me, I think he has more than enough Diocesan commitments. Anyway, I'll leave you in peace, Jennie.'

Bryn quietly closed the door and went down to his study to continue his sermon preparation. As he was about to leave for his meeting, 'Colin's Constructions' van drew up. Due to his many commitments he hadn't seen much of the workmen so he enquired how things were going.

'We're getting there mate,' replied Colin. 'It's one heck of a job though. Replacing a roof like this can sometimes take months.'

'Oh dear, I hope that it won't take that long,' replied Bryn. 'Brian Smith estimated four to five weeks and he's usually reasonably accurate. Anyway, thank you very much. I'll see you again.'

Bryn got into his car and left for his meeting.

'BBC..Radio1!!!!' Jennie woke suddenly to a blaring sound of pop music coming directly from outside the bedroom window. There was a tier of scaffolding surrounding the

upstairs level of the house; some weeks before Bryn had joked about the possibility of a peeping tom coming to give them the 'once over' as they rested in the privacy of their own home. She immediately felt extremely vulnerable, but the headache remained too intense for her to do anything apart from puff up her pillow and pull the duvet cover over her head.

'*Hoi!! Mate!! Look out!!* I'm chucking this down!' and there was a crashing sound that almost shook the house.

'That was a close shave Rick,' shouted Jonathan.

This was followed by loud laughter and rapport amongst the workmen. The radio continued to play loudly.

'Pump up the volume, will you, butt?' called Dave from the tier below. 'Can't hear nothing from down by 'ere.'

'*Yes! siree!!*' yelled Jonathan in as loud a voice as he could manage. 'This is one of my favourites.'

He began singing along at the top of his voice, adding percussion by means of stamping on the scaffolding and banging tools noisily together.

Gavin joined in with a deafening *'Ba! Ba! Ba! Baa! Ba! Ba! Ba! Ba Ba!!"* over and over again. 'Oh *yeah!*' he screeched when the number came to an end. 'Play it again, Sam.'

The men hadn't appeared for the previous two days as they had been carrying out emergency repairs at St. Non's Vicarage; Jennie was wishing that it had taken them just one day longer to complete the work there.

'Hoi, Rick! Come up here and have a look at this, mate,' Darren requested.

Despite the pain, Jennie lifted her head to check that the curtains were drawn tightly together.

'Rick! Mate!' screeched Darren, exercising his vocal chords to capacity. 'Can you hear me? Come up here. The sooner the better, so that I can get on with my work.'

'Oh, *please, please do*,' mouthed Jennie from beneath the duvet. Apparently he wanted to share with his colleague the message he had found in the fortune cookie that he had been given in his local Chinese Restaurant the previous evening. He had taken his wife Delyth to 'Panda's' to celebrate her twentieth birthday.

'What's up Dar?' enquired Rick from outside the bedroom window.

Darren proceeded to read out the declaration….'You will soon be confronted with *unlimited* possibilities. It's my fortune Rick. I'm going to join the upper classes. No more heavy work and long hours for me.'

He turned to face Jennie's bedroom window and not thinking for a moment that there was anybody near, he began to speak. 'Window, window on this house, tell me quiet like a mouse; If it's true don't say nowt, if it ain't then bang about.' He paused for a moment,' then said,' 'I'll give you sixty seconds.'

He began to count. By now Jennie had heard enough so, with all the strength she could muster at the time, she dragged herself out of bed, went to the window and gave it several robust raps.

'Hoi, Rick! Hear that? There must be a presence there. *Help!!*'

'Oh shut up Darren. You're not right in the head mate,' said Gavin. The game was over. 'Why don't you just get on with the job like the rest of us?'

After a lengthy pause Gavin asked 'Right, who's for a cuppa?'

Jennie could take no more, so she went into the small bedroom on the side of the house and slept for the rest of the morning. When she woke up, her migraine had cleared and she was feeling much better. She believed that she was more than able to cope, once again, with workmen and scaffolding. As she walked towards her own bedroom, she sensed tranquillity in the camp and assumed that the boys must be taking a lunch break. When she looked out of the window, however, the forecourt was empty; Colin's Constructors had awarded themselves a half day so, when Brian Smith came to do a quick survey later that afternoon, the workmen were nowhere to be seen.

'I thought I might have caught them before they left,' he said to Jennie. 'Anyway it looks like they're making excellent progress. I've given you the best of the bunch here Jennie, that's for sure.' Jennie thought it best that she kept her opinion to herself. She simply acknowledged his comments with a smile and a nod. However, by the end of that week the work was complete and on the Friday afternoon, at a quarter past two precisely, Bryn and Jennie waved a fond farewell to Colin and his sluggish squad, hoping that their services would not be required ever again.

'Thank you very much indeed,' said Bryn as Colin turned on the ignition. 'You've done a remarkable job on that roof!'

Jennie could not believe what Bryn was saying. There was no way that he could have seen the completed work for himself; she believed that there must have been some divine intervention to make him seem so certain. Later that afternoon Brian Smith telephoned to inform Bryn and Jennie that all being well, the scaffolding would be removed the following week. He also told them that he had arranged for John Thomas & Sons, Plasterers, to begin work in the bedroom first thing on Monday morning.

'*Do come in*,' said Jennie pleasantly as she opened the door to the workmen on that day. She was now convinced that there was indeed a light at the end of the tunnel.

'Sorry to tell you this, Mrs. Jenkins. We've only come for a look-see today but we'll be here tomorrow without fail. Oh, I'm John by the way and my apprentice in the van is Gareth. We've been called to do some emergency work in St. Non's Vicarage. Brian told us what he wanted done, but, if you don't mind, I'll take a peek. Seeing is believing so they say, not that I'm a Doubting Thomas.'

John was one of the very few workmen employed by the diocese who regularly attended a place of worship, although many of them claimed to be closer to God than even the most devout cleric, due to the fact that they spent much of their working hours at high altitudes. John went to view the work that was needed to be carried out in the bedroom and returned with good news for the waiting Jennie.

'One day's work should do it, then it will be up to the decorators,' he said, and he left for St. Non's Vicarage.

As Jennie sat down by the kitchen table, her thoughts were of the Reverend Timothy Christopher and his continual emergency requirements. He frequently made mountains out of molehills and always responded to everything in the extreme. The fact that he had performed with the Royal Shakespeare Company before becoming ordained might have contributed to this. Jennie thought that he was very highly strung and was in desperate need of a wife.

At 8:15a.m. the following day Gareth and Les were ringing the doorbell.

'*Do come in,*' said Jennie. 'I see John isn't with you today.'

'He's at St. Non's completing emergency work,' replied Les. 'He dropped us off here on his way.'

'Amen, so be it' thought Jennie but said nothing. 'If there's anything that I can do to help, then don't be afraid to ask,' she said assuredly, as the young men made their way to the bedroom with the intention, she hoped, of sorting out the problem once and for all.

After a short while she called to them from the hallway. 'Everything alright?'

'Well, yes and no,' came the reply.

'What do you mean by that?'

'The work is going fine, but we left our boxes in John's transit.'

'Do the boxes contain any necessary equipment?' she asked.

'Aye, you bet! We left our sandwich boxes in it, so we haven't got no dinner, nor nothing for our breaks,' replied Gareth. 'I'm bloody devastated, if you don't mind my saying so.'

'Watch your language butt,' said Les. 'You're not in the rugby club now.'

'No problem,' said Jennie. 'I'll fix some sandwiches for lunch and some portions of fruit. Help yourselves to tea or coffee here in the kitchen. The storage jars are clearly marked. I have to attend a funeral in Llanmaldwyn at mid-day.' Mrs. Lisa Evans, enrolling member of the Mothers' Union branch there for over forty years all told, would have turned one hundred and six had she continued breathing for a further three and a half hours. I'll be leaving in about thirty minutes, but everything will be prepared by then. The used crockery can go in the dishwasher. Maybe I'll see you when I get back. Bryn has a meeting in the Deanery. I doubt if he'll be back much before seven thirty this evening. I expect you'll be done and dusted by then, so I shouldn't think you'll see him on this occasion. Never mind; he's doing very well, sitting up and taking notice and all that jazz! I'll say a premature cheerio and, by the way, thanks a bunch.'

Gareth and Les had finished the plastering a long time before Jennie returned from Llanmaldwyn. They had left a note for her on the kitchen table thanking her for the hospitality and informing her that Brian Smith had called by. A couple of the lads from Colin's Constructions would be available for the remainder of the inside work from the following Tuesday. The plastering would be thoroughly dried out by then. Jennie was hoping that neither Darren nor Gavin would be involved in the impending painting and decorating; they worked too slowly and half heartedly for her liking, particularly when Colin, the foreman was not present.

At about 9:30 the following Tuesday morning, Bryn left the vicarage to celebrate the 10 o' clock Eucharist at St. Mary Magdalene and from there he was going to do some visiting, including a trip to Nant -y- Mynydd Nursing Home to see Idris Williams and to take him the Eucharist. This would mean that Bryn would be out until mid - afternoon at the earliest.

Shortly after they had said their 'goodbyes' the doorbell rang. Jennie hurried to the door, assuming that Bryn must have forgotten his keys. As she opened the door she saw two very familiar faces. The two lads allocated to the task were none other than the idle duo.

'*Do come in*,' said Jennie with a radiant smile. She hadn't been a drama teacher for nothing! 'I'll show you which bedroom it is and then I'll leave you to it.'

'Any chance of a cuppa before we start?' asked Gavin.

'Aye, that sounds good,' added Darren as he pointed to the downstairs cloakroom, nodded and disappeared. He was on familiar ground.

Jennie thought it best that they should help themselves to beverages, so she took six teabags from the tea caddy and placed them on a saucer on the worktop, along with milk and sugar and a few digestive biscuits. She was sure that three cups per head would be more than sufficient for their needs. She herself, being editor of the diocesan Mothers' Union journal, was attempting to meet the deadline for printing at the end of the week and there was no time to lose. It was imperative that all the announcements that she had been sent would appear in the subsequent issue. Mrs. Mary Evans from the parish of Derwen Fawr, for example, would not appreciate having her 100th birthday congratulations in three months time, when the next edition would be published, and by then Mrs. Elizabeth Stowell's baby, Eli Wyn, would have outgrown his newborn wardrobe at the vicarage in the parish of Bro Celynen.

As Jennie walked into the study to use the computer she heard Radio One blaring away upstairs. She selected Handel's Messiah from the CD rack at the side of Bryn's desk and put on the Halleluiah Chorus at ear- splitting volume and, if she could have pumped it up a bit more, then she would have done so gladly. She began her work, always scrutinising the names and the corresponding columns; after all, placing the names of new members in the obituary column, as she had done in her first periodical, was an episode never to be repeated!

Darren and Gavin had completed the decorating by mid-afternoon the next day and Jennie was very pleased with the end product. She had opened the door to let them in at about 9 o' clock that morning but she herself had left the premises soon after to go to the printer's, then she had met up with a friend in Llanelfed for lunch. She returned to the vicarage at about 3:30 p.m and by then the workmen had gone. Jennie decided to arrange the bedroom as tidily as possible and then went downstairs to prepare the evening meal, knowing that they should not be inconvenienced by workmen or scaffolding for the foreseeable future.

This was indeed, a red letter day for St. Mary Magdalene Vicarage. She couldn't hide her excitement when Bryn came home later that afternoon.

'Shall we drink a toast to the departed?' she asked as she poured each of them a generous glass of claret. 'After all, I'm not expecting to see them again.'

Jennie hoped that from now on the only workmen she would be aware of would be those engaged in road maintenance…. and as for the scaffolding … well, she would be more inclined to attempt to climb Jacob's ladder any day.

However, the scaffolding was not dismantled until six weeks later!

Chapter 5: MID-SUMMER LUNCHES

Parochial Church Council meetings were held on the last Thursday of the month at 7:30 p.m. They were generally well attended and Bryn was pleased that most of the members took their responsibilities seriously. There were one or two whom he thought could contribute a little more whilst present at the meeting, instead of discussing topics as they were leaving the premises, and there were some individuals whom he believed should exercise a little more restraint, but in the main most were supportive of his ideas. This year's Easter Vestry Meeting had been particularly successful, and his suggestion in the 'A.O.B' part of the agenda, of an icon placed in the nave, as a stimulant to prayer was accepted without question. He was hoping that the suggestions he would offer tonight would meet with similar acceptance.

Dr. Huw Martin was to give a short resume from the meeting of the Diocesan Council and Mrs. Beryl Francis was to report on the Mothers' Union Conference, but the only item on the agenda for actual discussion this evening would be the Summer Fund-Raising Event. Every year, even before Bryn had been inducted into the parish of St. Mary Magdalene, a fund raising event had been held in the summer, mainly to enhance church funds and enable the paying of the quota to be a manageable possibility.

Bryn organised several charity events during the year including the Christian Aid walk around the parish boundaries and the walk from Horeb Chapel to Maesgwyn Farm to raise money for those afflicted with Aids. There had also been a very successful auction when almost £950 had been raised for an Emergency Overseas Appeal. The Sunday School's five hour silence in aid of children in the Darfur province of Africa had raised a goodly sum, as had the Mothers' Union Coffee Morning in aid of a new branch in the out-backs of Tanzania. It was fair to say that parishioners gave of their all when it came to raising money.

The Summer Fund Raising Event was different in so much as the monies raised on this occasion were for church funds only. Some years ago the parish was able to purchase a complete dinner set for one hundred people, along with cutlery and glasses, and still have money in hand to pay for the quota. This was due to the fact that on that occasion the Church Fayre had been opened by Dame Hettie Meredith, a former resident of the village, who had given a cheque amounting to a five figure sum as a donation to the event.

For two years the Mothers' Union had organised a Strawberry Tea. Unfortunately they had chosen to hold it on the same day as the Ordination Service held in the Cathedral in St. Deiniol's. Bryn's loyalties lay at both and two years ago, more by luck than judgement, having made the fifty five mile journey back to Rhydbrychan in record time, he had walked through the doors of the church hall, just in time to hear his name being announced as winner of the first prize in the raffle.

'Congratulations Vicar,' said Meirion. 'You've won first prize. Shall I open the envelope to reveal what it is?'

'Yes please,' replied Bryn, closing the doors behind him.

He was, to all intent and purposes feeling somewhat flustered and slightly irritable if truth were known.

'What a magnificent prize!' said Meirion as he withdrew the small card to reveal the award. 'It's a weekend break for two at Awel-y-Mor' which was a three star hotel in Trehyfryd.

It had been very kindly donated by Mrs. Bronwen Edwards, the proprietor, and sister of Mrs. Pat Lewis.

Bryn's little grey cells began to work overtime. Trehyfryd was about a five mile walk from Rhydbrychan - quite within his capabilities - and to lose one Sunday out of the four to which he was entitled during the year seemed to be a bit of a waste. Glancing at some of the bottles that were on display he wished that he had won the port instead. He smiled benignly and said, 'Thank you very much, but I'd like you to redraw.'

Instead the prize went to a delighted Mrs. Ida Phillips.

Last year's *BBQ* had been a wash out due to the inclement weather and both Huw Martin and Meirion Lloyd, who had been unanimously elected as chefs for that occasion, were rooting for something completely different this year.

Bryn sat at his desk in the study looking at the notes he had prepared for the meeting that was to be held in about an hour's time. He felt quite excited at the prospect he had in mind, and although it would mean a lot of hard work and cooperation on behalf of the parishioners, he felt certain that the event would prove to be a resounding success. He was going to suggest a Flower Festival. This would be something entirely new for the parish and he felt quite confident that his suggestion would not meet with any opposition, so at

7:20 p.m. he left the vicarage and made the short walk to the church hall. At 7:30 p.m. he opened the meeting with prayer and then went on to thank everyone for attending.

Apologies were received from Lucy Richards, who was participating in a Musical Evening with the local WI, and from Mr. Charles Harris, whose car had broken down on the mountain near Cwmdu Farm. He was waiting for the fourth emergency service to arrive when he had telephoned Meirion.

'The engine just seemed to fizzle out,' he had reported, 'so give my apologies if you will.'

'By all means Charles,' Meirion had replied. 'By the way, do you have any suggestions for the fund raiser?'

'I most certainly do. How about the Mothers' Union doing a Beachwear Fashion Show? That should bring in mega bucks! Thanks pal. Bye for now,' and he had rung off leaving Meirion to conjure up some very vivid pictures in his mind.

When the reports from the Diocesan Council and the Mothers' Union Conference had been read and applauded and Bryn, on behalf of the parish, had thanked Huw and Beryl for their support, he went on to say,

'As you can see, it is most important that we, as a parish, play an active part in Diocesan activities. In this way we have a clear understanding of what is taking place within the diocese and the implications it may have for us as a parish. However, we will now move on to the only other item on this evening's agenda which is of course The Summer Fundraising Event. Are there any suggestions or comments?'

Huw Martin raised his hand, 'I propose that we do *not* have a *BBQ.* this year.'

'I'll second that!' said Meirion. 'Let's have something that can be held indoors so that it can be a case of never mind the weather as long as we're together!' He laughed audibly.

'Point taken,' said Bryn, nodding his head in agreement and knowing that he himself had an excellent indoor event to suggest. He did not want to rush into things, however, and it was only fair for the parochial church council members to have their say. 'Anyone else?' asked Bryn. Meirion refrained from mentioning the suggestion offered to him by Charles Harris, but he couldn't help but smile to himself as he looked in the direction of Lillian Shanks and imagined her parading down the catwalk in a swimsuit.

'How about a Summer Eisteddfod?' suggested Mrs. Ida Phillips. 'There's a lot of talent in the village. I'm sure that people from St Catherine's and St. Edward's would join in too.' She paused expectantly, 'What do you think Vicar?'

'The thing is Mrs. Phillips, we want to make as much money as we can. With a competition there would have to be prizes.'

'People would pay to enter of course and perhaps the winners could have a certificate only. Surely any adjudicators would give their services free of charge. We could sell refreshments and have a raffle to boost funds.'

The fact that Ida Phillips had been practicing 'All in the April Evening' with the intention of taking part in the 'over seventy fives' solo competition that would surely be included in the programme, was known only to herself and to her Maker.

'What do you think Vicar?' she asked again.

'I can see Meirion is making notes of the suggestions being made,' he said tactfully, 'so maybe we can take a vote later. Thank you Mrs. Phillips.'

A short silence followed, so Bryn assumed that there were no more ideas forthcoming.

'Well,' he said with a smile, 'if there are no more suggestions I would like to put forward my idea of a......' He noticed a raised hand. It belonged to Mrs. Lillian Shanks. 'I'm sorry Mrs. Shanks. I see that you would like to make a contribution.'

'That's alright Vicar. It can wait. We'll hear your suggestion first. Go ahead please.'

'I thought that this year's fundraiser could be a Flower Festival. It would be held right here in church of course, and perhaps there could be activities going on in the church hall at the same time. It could be officially opened on a Thursday perhaps and could run until the Sunday Evening, ending with a 'Songs of Praise'. This could be followed by a Cheese and Wine in the vicarage. A special Eucharist could be held and maybe Bishop Anselm or the Archdeacon would be available to preach, and we could arrange a children's service based on the theme. We must have a theme of course.'

Ken Thomas immediately raised his hand. 'What an excellent idea Vicar.' He paused. 'How about 'The Church's Year' as a theme? I saw it done in a church in Bedford Park in

London a few years ago and it was spectacular. I was deeply moved by all the wonderful floral displays there. They were both thought provoking and awe inspiring. Yes, Vicar...The Church's Year would be my suggestion.'

'That's a good theme,' added Chris Pugh. 'We can use what's left of the Advent Candle. It's in the right hand cupboard in the vestry. The crib is under the table and all the figures should be there. Ah!, on second thoughts, did anyone have the savvy to stick Joseph's head back on after that bad kick he had in the sanctuary at the Epiphany service? I guess we'll have to look into that.'

'Thank you both, but I thought that perhaps we could give ourselves a greater challenge and although I think that 'The Church's Year' is an excellent idea may I suggest the theme 'Pillars of Faith' based on our Old Testament Heritage. We would have a wealth of characters from whom to chose, including Daniel in the Lions' Den and Joseph and his multi-coloured coat and of course, the Boy Samuel. But before we get carried away, as it were, I believe that Mrs. Shanks had a suggestion to make.'

'Indeed I do Vicar,' she replied with confidence. 'Although I believe that each of the suggestions made here this evening is valid and possible - yours included if I may be bold enough to say so - I feel that what I am about to suggest will take us one step further as parishioners..... as villagers......as a serving community if you like.'

Lillian addressed the members present as if she, herself, was 'in the chair'.

She continued. 'We have an obligation in this place. As we are told in the Bible, we must be doers not hearers only, though its actual reference escapes me at this particular moment in time. I believe that we have a duty to reach out to the community of which we are a part. After all, isn't that what we should be doing as Christians in this place, at this time?' She paused.

Assuming, rightly, that Mrs. Shanks had completed her soliloquy Bryn tentatively enquired, 'and what is your suggestion, Mrs. Shanks?' There was a slight buzz amongst the gathering.

'Midsummer lunches,' came the reply.

A complete silence fell over those present. People were either afraid to speak, or they were waiting to hear more. Mrs. Lillian Shanks repeated 'I suggest Midsummer Lunches.' She breathed deeply. 'Midsummer Lunches......You all know, as well as I do, how very successful both the Advent Soup Lunches and the Lenten Bread and Cheese Lunches have been over the years. We have made a lot of money for Charities and all events were greatly supported, as well as being wonderful social occasions. Therefore, Ladies and Gentlemen, Vicar, I suggest that this year's Summer Fundraising Event be Midsummer Lunches, being provided in the same manner as Advent Lunches, that is, over a four week period, though not on four consecutive weeks of course. That would be too exhausting for the helpers and the lunches might well lose their impact. Thank you for listening.'

'I'll second that one,' said Chris Pugh. 'At least it will save me worrying about what Phil and I will have for food for four days over the period. We can just turn up and be served!'

'My *dear* Christine,' said Mrs. Shanks, 'I'm sure that we shall all be expecting you to help out with kitchen duties if at all possible.'

'Love one another as God has loved you!' thought Chris, but said nothing.

Mrs. Hilda Grey raised her hand to speak. 'Excuse me please, Vicar,' she said. 'I think that both the idea of a Flower Festival and the suggestion of the Midsummer Lunches are quite unique and *so* different. They are both excellent suggestions, so do you think that we should have a show of hands to decide?'

'In a moment, perhaps, Hilda.'

In his heart of hearts Bryn was bidding 'farewell' to the Pillars of Faith and his Old Testament heritage until the following year at least. His only chance of winning now was if Lillian Shanks had given insufficient thought to the implementation of her idea. It would definitely need greater organisation than the Advent and the Lenten Lunches, and a much more varied menu.

'Thank you Mrs. Shanks for such an interesting contribution. Do you feel able to explain to the P.C.C. how these lunches could be arranged?'

'I most certainly do, Vicar. One example would be a roast dinner - not necessarily on a Sunday of course. Let me suggest' - and she paused for a moment to refer to the small notepad that she was removing from the black leather handbag that people had come to regard as her soul mate. 'I've made a few notes here, but as you all know I'm always open to ideas, so please stop me if you have anything that you need to say urgently.'

Nobody, including Bryn - or even Bishop Anselm, had he been party to proceedings - would have the audacity to stop Mrs. Lillian Shanks in mid-flow.

'My suggestion is as follows… The Midsummer Lunches could be held on four occasions, sometime between early June and the end of July. Menus would be varied and, as I said a moment ago, one meal could be a roast, three courses of course - pardon the pun! Another lunch could take the form of a ham salad, with starters and dessert to be arranged. The third week could be, perhaps melon as a first course, followed by pasta dishes with cheese and biscuits to finish, and I thought that perhaps our final Midsummer Lunch could take on the form of a *Buffet Magnifique*, with as many as possible of us bringing along our very own favourite dishes. They would need to be of a very high standard, of course. By that I mean no burnt quiches, no semi-hard boiled eggs, neither any eggs with black rings for that matter, no flat Victoria sponge cakes and absolutely no rock cakes! We've all been there and done it and worn the T- shirt, so you all know what I'm talking about. Thank you, Vicar, that is all,' and on that final note of her notes she sat down.

'Thank you Mrs. Shanks, for the superb contribution that you have made to this evening's meeting.'

He surveyed the church council with a genuine smile and said, 'I propose that we take on this challenge of the Midsummer Lunches as our parish Summer Fundraising Event for this year. Do we have a seconder?'

'I'll second that,' said Chris Pugh eagerly. 'I love the sound of the Buffet Magnifique. You know me, see food and eat it!'

Had she genuinely been worth her weight in gold, then perhaps the parish of St. Mary Magdalene would have no need to discuss fundraising efforts at all.

'All in favour?' asked the Chair.

'Aye!' came a unanimous reply, comparable perhaps to the Prime Minister's proclamation of an increased pay deal for all Members of Parliament!

'I trust that you're not going to take this personally Vicar,' said Mrs. Shanks. 'Quite possibly we can have a Flower Festival next year. All in favour?'

'Aye!'

So much clapping and cheering followed that nobody heard the croaky voice of Mrs. Ida Phillips enquiring about a possible date for the Eisteddfod.

It was decided that Mrs. Lillian Shanks would assume overall responsibility for the Midsummer Lunches, along with a small committee of volunteers who would assist with arrangements. Those interested in helping were asked to put their names forward during the coming week, and Bryn would make an announcement at the Sunday Eucharist. He thanked everyone for attending the meeting and expressed his delight that so much had been achieved. He had been very impressed with the enthusiasm of all those present and their readiness to contribute to and participate in the suggestions made. It had, indeed been a very fruitful meeting, but for now, he requested that everyone focus on the forthcoming fundraising event, which was to be the Midsummer Lunches. Members joined in the saying of 'The Grace' together before making their way home.

As Bryn locked the church hall door he was feeling positively elated. It was true to say that this had been one of the most successful meetings of the Parochial Church Council that he had chaired during his ministry. He remembered the time, in a former parish, when only three members had turned up for the meeting that had been called to consider the implementation of the new Eucharist Service. Maybe people had been voting with their feet. This evening they had been voting with their hearts and hands and voices - albeit for a series of Midsummer Lunches suggested by Mrs. Lillian Shanks, as opposed to a Flower Festival suggested by the Incumbent, but Bryn had no hard feelings. 'Better the devil you know than the devil you don't,' he thought in the nicest possible way. In fact he was very fond of Mrs. Lillian Shanks and felt that what one saw of Lillian was not the whole Lillian. Maybe, one day, she would remove the mask as it were, but, until she was ready to do so, then it would be a case of 'what you see is what you get'.

As Bryn made his way down the path he could see the head of someone on the other side of the boundary wall. A hand waved. As he got nearer the gate he could see that it was Mrs. Shanks.

'Excuse me Vicar, but I couldn't possibly go home without congratulating you on an excellent meeting. I think that it was probably the best church meeting that I have ever attended. It was certainly the best to which I have ever contributed. Everybody seemed so supportive. Just one thing seems to have been overlooked, Vicar, if you don't mind my saying so.'

'What is that Mrs. Shanks?' he enquired. 'I thought that we had covered just about everything.'

'Apart from following up Mrs. Ida Phillips' suggestion of an Eisteddfod.' She paused. 'Hardly a fundraiser, if I may be so bold to comment.'

'I'm sure that we can have such an event at some time during our social calendar. I'll certainly give it some thought.'

'Not tonight, I hope, Vicar. I think we've all thought enough for one evening. Goodnight.'

At that point, and with head held high, Lillian made a sharp turn to the right and Bryn walked toward the vicarage.

'Goodnight Mrs. Shanks, and thank you for everything.'

Even if she *did* hear him, there was no reply.

As Bryn walked through the vicarage door he was met by a delicious smell of meat roasting in the oven. He felt absolutely exhausted by now, wanting just a cup of tea to revive him and perhaps one of Beryl's welshcakes if there were any left. He hoped that Jennie would remain occupied because the last thing he wanted now was an inquisition into this evening's P.C.C. Suffice for him to tell Jennie that he had lost 16-1 to Mrs. Lillian Shanks.

'Hello love. I hope you're not too disappointed,' called Jennie from the kitchen.

Bryn could hardly believe his ears. Disappointed? How had she heard the outcome of the meeting so quickly and, moreover, he was not disappointed at all. He was more than delighted with the way that events had worked out.

'Why should I be disappointed Jennie?' he asked as he walked into the kitchen.

'Well, this lovely smell greeting you as you came in. It's not for now; it's for tomorrow as I'll be out most of the day. Remember I mentioned that I was taking flowers to the cemetery and then visiting my cousin? Well, as you know, it's a hundred and fifty mile round trip so I thought that I'd better cook this rib of beef tonight. As I said, I hope that you're not disappointed. I'll make a nice pot of tea in a moment and I think that there are three or four of Beryl's welshcakes left in the tin.'

Bryn's eyes lit up, and he beamed - who could ask for *anything* more? As they sat together sipping tea at the kitchen table Jennie began to eulogise on an idea that had struck her appertaining to the Flower Festival.

'I have to take my hat off to you, Bryn,' she said, 'but the more I think about it the more I consider it to be one of your best ideas yet, the Flower Festival I mean. Well, during the time that you have been sorting it all out - and I don't suppose you've left any stones unturned - I've been coming up with my own suggestion. I think that it is achievable, although I say it myself. (She was only joking of course, but Bryn wasn't to know that.) Would it be possible, in fact, would it be *at all* possible, to include real people amongst the displays? Well, by that I mean one display. I'll be responsible for it if you like… .but I was thinking how much more meaningful "The Boy Samuel" would be if we were able to include a real live Samuel and a real live Eli.'

Jennie was becoming increasingly excited. 'I don't mean that anyone should remain as part of the display for the duration of the Festival; I thought perhaps a two hour rota, since they're supposed to be sleeping most of the time anyway. Maybe Father Jeffrey and young Robert could start off, followed perhaps by Meirion or Huw. Personally, I don't think that Charles Harris is a suitable Eli, but it's up to you of course, you're the boss... well here at St. Mary Magdalene, I mean. I'm sure that we would have no end of volunteers. We could put a list up in the church porch. What do you think *Vicar?*'

He had heard that somewhere before and not so long ago.

'I think, my dearest, that it is probably one of the most original ideas ever offered as part of a Flower Festival. However, our Flower Festival has been postponed until next year.'

Jennie looked at him in disbelief. She, only she, was aware of the hours he had spent in planning and research. She, only she, had already done a proof- reading of a flyer asking for volunteers to man the church, provide refreshments, and offer help in so many other aspects during the Festival Weekend. Apart from actually placing flowers at the foot of the pulpit she knew that Bryn was more than ready to portray 'Isaiah's Dream' - this is what he had chosen as his personal contribution. Jennie sat in stunned silence as she tried to fathom out what had caused the change of heart.

'Could it be....could it be that there were not enough members to make a quorum?' she asked eventually.

'All present and correct, in fact, apart from the apologies received from Lucy and Charles Harris.'

'Then why no Flower Festival? Much as I love these folk I doubt if anyone came up with anything better.'

'Well, actually there was another suggestion that seemed to be more appropriate for us as a parish here and now.'

Jennie waited in anticipation. Secretly her thoughts were running between Eli and Samuel, strawberry teas, barbecues and treasure hunts, along perhaps, with a bottle stall for the over eighteens. 'There's no way that I can even attempt to guess at this, I'll have to hear it from the horse's mouth.'

Bryn walked towards the cake tin and eyed it up and down before speaking.

'Jennie Jenkins,' he said with authority. 'It gives me great pleasure to inform you that this year's fundraising event is to take the form of Midsummer Lunches. It was suggested by Mrs. Lillian Shanks, proposed by me, seconded by Mrs. Chris Pugh and unanimously accepted. Mrs. Shanks went on to stress the importance of reaching out to the community and she has a point there. She had obviously put a great deal of thought and effort into her suggestion.'

'But so had you, Bryn, *so had you!* You've spent hours upon hours working on Pillars of Faith.'

'There is a strong possibility that we can do that next year. As for now, we must don our chefs' caps and butchers' aprons and prepare for the Midsummer Lunches. By the way, Lillian is hoping for some volunteers to help with arrangements.'

'Of course I'll help......albeit on one condition. Am I right in thinking that these lunches are to be served in the church hall? As you so frequently say, there's only room for *one* cook in the kitchen!'

'Absolutely Jennie. The venue will be clearly printed on the tickets.'

It was decided that the Midsummer Lunches would take place in the parish hall of St. Mary Magdalene on Wednesday 6th June, Thursday 21st June, Friday 6th July and Sunday 22nd July. Mr. Charles Harris was responsible for publicity and the printing of 'dinner' tickets. It was unanimously decided that each lunch would include three courses, along with tea, coffee and soft drinks. Tickets would be sold at a cost of £5 for adults and £3.50 for children. There would be no concessions for senior citizens. Wine would be served only at the Buffet Magnifique, and at a very moderate charge of 50 pence a glass. Everything, it seemed was going to plan. Lillian suggested that the Men's Society might like to be in complete charge of the lunch arranged for Thursday 21st of June, thus giving herself and her team a chance to sit and be served.

At the Sunday Eucharist, prior to the start of the series of Midsummer Lunches, Bryn expressed how delighted he was to hear that there were only a few tickets remaining for the first venture, which was, as he reminded everyone, only days away.

At the same time as he was speaking in the church, Lucy Richards was trying to get the oven to light in the church hall. Her Sunday School lesson had been based on the feeding of the five thousand (John 6) and the importance of sharing, so her class had been making cakes to share with the congregation at coffee time, which was held immediately after the service. Because her class had been so responsive, she had promised to boil some milk for them to have a drink of hot chocolate as a change from the weak orange juice that was generally provided each Sunday. The automatic ignition on the stove had died a death several years before, but the escape of gas had responded successfully to a lighted match ever since.......or rather, until now.

Today, however, it seemed as though the complete appliance needed some sort of rehab. Not even Uncle James, the Sunday School Superintendent, could raise a flash, and he being generally regarded as a Jack of all trades!

'Its life is over Lucy,' he said in a melancholy tone of voice. 'It's had a good innings. If my memory serves me correctly it was installed when I was wearing short trousers and old Mr. Sweet was selling sherbet lemons. Well, I don't know if his name was really Mr. Sweet or if we just called him that! Anyway, that's enough reminiscing. We've got something very serious on our hands here.' He lit a match and tried the hob, but there was no response there either. He blew out the match and tried the oven again, then again and yet again. He made one final attempt before admitting that his efforts had been in vain.

'It is with a heavy heart, Lucy, that I pronounce that this gas cooker is non-operational, obsolete and completely dysfunctional. In other words, its life is over. Amen. So be it.' Out of respect to the cooker and to the utility to which it is assigned he omitted the '*Alleluia*.'

Lucy explained the problem to the children, many of whom had already made their own assessments.

'Would you like me to take the cakes over to my house to cook?' asked Sally helpfully. She lived directly opposite the church. 'I know that Mum's in the service, but Dad's at home. He's on the internet I expect.'

'Thank you very much,' replied Lucy, handing Sally two patty tins. 'Who would like to give Sally a hand and carry *these* two patty tins over to her kitchen?'

Gemma put up her hand.

'Thanks Gem. It's gas mark 4 for 15-20 minutes, so they should be just ready by the end of the Eucharist.'

Sally and Gemma had left the building before you could say 'Jack Robinson.' However, this obsolete cooker had far-reaching implications of course, not least of all for the impending Midsummer Lunches, and coffee and home made cakes were to be served the following morning after the Mothers' Union Deanery Festival. That stalwart, that modern day pillar of the church, had a lot to answer for. How inconsiderate of it to give up the ghost at such a busy time. It just enhanced the belief that humans are far superior to inanimate objects any day!

Sally and Gemma arrived at the back of the church just as the service was drawing to a close. Sally's father had managed to tear himself from the www.co.uks in order to find some paper plates on which to serve the cakes. He himself had almost burnt his mouth as he took one directly from the patty tin.

'Can I have a quick word please Bryn?' asked James, as he met him coming out of the vestry. 'The cooker is obsolete.

Its life is over. Can you spare a moment to come and have a look?'

'Of course I can,' replied Bryn, 'but surely it's not *that* old. I thought it was installed shortly before I came.'

'Vicar, it was installed when I was wearing short trousers and I hadn't even had a swimming lesson.'

James was now the senior swimming instructor at the local recreation centre. Having lit almost twenty matches, and having almost burnt each of the fingers on his right hand in the process Bryn agreed, regrettably, that the appliance had become obsolete. They returned to the church together and Bryn proceeded quickly to the tables at the back, where he picked up a spoon and rapped it vigorously against a saucer.

'First of all, I'm sure that you would like to join me in thanking Lucy and her class for these lovely cakes that have been freshly made for us all to enjoy with our coffee. We all know how important it is to share.' He smiled at the youngsters. 'I'm glad to see that there's one left for me. Thank you too, to young Sally here, without whom these cakes would not have been possible.'

Having no idea as to what had been going on her mother, Hilda Grey was completely nonplussed.

'To cut a long story short, the cooker in the church hall has packed in, consequently the Midsummer Lunches and tomorrow's Mothers' Union coffee and cakes will be held at the vicarage. Please would you pass this information on by word of mouth? Thank you all very much.'

Although Jennie called a cheery 'goodbye' to Mrs. Lillian Shanks, Pat and others as she walked through the west door, she left the church with a heavy heart, knowing that her home would not be her own until at least after the last of the Midsummer Lunches. Bryn had placed his week's commitments on the fridge, by means of a souvenir magnet from Sorrento, and clearly there would be no time to look around for a new cooker for the church hall, and there would certainly be no time to negotiate its delivery and installation. Moreover, Jennie knew that for three days and two nights of the following week Bryn was away at a provincial conference. Duties for the week after that were hitherto sketchy, but she knew that Bryn would be away overnight on the Monday and Tuesday as part of his Board of Mission duties. A new cooker for the church hall would be the least of his concerns. She felt that she would have to come to terms with the fact that she must be, out of necessity the 'hostess with the *mostest*' (excluding Chris Pugh) and hand over the vicarage kitchen to the Midsummer Lunches coordinator.

Shortly after she had put the potatoes on to boil Bryn came into the kitchen. He hadn't stopped off in the study en route, as was his custom, because he still held his briefcase in his hand. He could see by the look on her face that she was not amused, so he tried to enlighten the situation by saying,

'Jennie, my dear, the Lord giveth and the Lord taketh away.'

She knew exactly what he was implying.

'That's all very well,' she replied, 'but I wish that He could have waited until after these Midsummer Lunches,' and she went on to recite the first few verses of Psalm 57 – 'Have mercy on me, O God, have mercy on me, for in you my soul takes refuge. I will take refuge in the shadow of your wings until the disaster has passed' adding ' and with that I will gird up my loins and a wonderful time will be had by all!'

The evening before the first of the lunches was due to be served, Jennie had managed to set twenty five places - restaurant style. She knew more tickets than that had been sold, but some people could eat outside on the patio and some perhaps in the Summer House. The weatherman, mentioning no names, had forecast a sunny day with temperatures well above average for the time of year, and the high pressure was expected to continue well into the beginning of July. Since Bryn was in the study when she received this news she lurched towards the television screen and gave the man in question an enormous kiss - not once, but twice! Her gratitude both to him and the Lord, was immeasurable.

Mrs. Lillian Shanks had arranged to arrive at the vicarage at 10 o' clock on the morning of Wednesday 6th June and at 10:00 a.m. precisely the vicarage doorbell rang.

'*Do come in*,' said Jennie. 'How lovely to see you. Here, let me help,' and she picked up four very heavy plastic bags that had been left by the front door. She called to Bryn who was working in the study. 'Another pair of hands please!'

Everything had been brought into the kitchen in record time, including tins of grapefruit, several legs of lamb and at least a dozen lamb chops, all of which were to be placed in the oven on a low gas or in the rayburn. The microwave was to be used only as a last resort. Since the meat had come directly from her own oven, Lillian wanted it to continue cooking slowly until the meal was going to be served.

'Is there anything I can do to help?' asked Jennie.

'Plenty, my dear. Could we possibly start with the potatoes? Don't peel them; we don't have that sort of time on our hands, but wash them thoroughly if you will. Thank you dear.'

Jennie was beginning to wonder if she was in her own kitchen or if she was treading on alien soil. She glanced over towards the 'mug tree' and saw the mug dedicated to the 'world's greatest husband' and felt that she must be on home ground after all. The fact that she could see her repeat prescription dangling on the refrigerator only endorsed these beliefs. The doorbell rang again.

'*Do come in*,' called Jennie again. 'The door *is* open.'

In came May and Helen. 'Ready to help,' they said in unison, as they gave a military salute.

They had obviously rehearsed their mode of entry in order to alleviate some of the stress that they thought might be prevalent in the kitchen at that time.

'Good morning both,' said Mrs. Shanks. 'This is going to be a very busy time for all of us,' and she suddenly began to sing the first few bars of 'Bind us together, Lord.' The volunteers glanced at each other in amazement.

Assuming the role of head chef, she spoke to mother and daughter. 'May, my dear, would you be so kind as to oversee the roast potatoes, cabbage and green beans and Helen, I'm putting you in charge of carrots and gravy. Any questions?'

'As a matter of fact, Mum and I were wondering if you wanted any table decorations? If so, we have more than enough in the car. We brought them just in case.'

Mrs. Lillian Shanks eyed Helen up and down almost to the point of embarrassment, though the embarrassment had more to do with Lillian Shanks than it had to do with Helen. Lillian, in her enthusiasm to provide a gourmet lunch that would be served perfectly had completely forgotten about table centres.

'Do place them on the tables please, dear. The aesthetic aspect can be completely and utterly your domain. Thank you.' She paused momentarily. 'Would you mind cutting up the cabbage as thinly as possible please May? It cooks better that way, and please do not forget to add bicarbonate of soda. We don't want to serve anything that is sub-standard. Everything must be palatable. Would you also make sure that the roast potatoes do not become subject to cremation? Thank you. You may proceed with your duties.'

It was about 11:30 when the doorbell rang again.

'*Do come in*,' called Jennie from the hallway.

It was Chris Pugh. She always had a Wednesday afternoon free, as it were, for lesson planning purposes and marking sessions and it was the policy of the school that this work could be carried out either at school or at the individual teacher's home. Chris preferred to work at home, but had stopped off to support the Midsummer Lunch en route. She walked straight into the kitchen.

'What a lovely smell of cooking. Are we having a tasting session?'

'Do you like grapefruit Christine?' asked Lillian Shanks.

'As a matter of fact I don't. It's one of the few things, the *very* few things, that I don't like.' 'In that case would you please place a serving in each of the bowls on the worktop and put one at each place setting? That would be very helpful. Thank you dear.'

Chris Pugh carried out the instructions to the best of her ability. If there was one short then she would send Phil over to the chip shop and he could have a rissole as a starter. Maybe she would send him over anyway, to fetch a battered cod that she could have as a fish course due to the fact that she disliked the grapefruit provided.

Just before 12:30 people began to arrive for the inaugural Midsummer Luncheon. Mrs. Beryl Francis apologised for not being able to help due to a doctor's appointment, but she was more than willing to assist with the clearing up afterwards.

'Fine,' said Lillian Shanks. 'There's always plenty to do at a time like this dear. Jennie has assured me that there's plenty of hot water and I can see a new bottle of washing up liquid by the sink. I believe that there may be a few utensils ready for washing as we speak. Take a look, dear, maybe there is something that you can be getting on with as of now!'

Owain Rogers was the next to arrive, accompanied by his wife Jane, the local lollipop lady.

'My dear Jane, I certainly didn't expect to see you here at the lunch,' said Lillian Shanks. 'I would consider this time of day to be one of the prime times of your employment. I hope the school children all remember the rules of the Green

Cross Code. You don't think you're risking it, dear, if you see what I mean?'

'Marian Fowler's doing my shift today. I'm sure you know her. She's got four children, three boys and a girl all by different fathers. Anyway, she's met Mr. Right now and I think that she's going to have a word with Bryn about getting married in church and having a white wedding, the choir, bells and everything else. If you don't know who I'm talking about slip over to the chip shop between 4:00 and 6:00 today because she's working then as well.' However Lillian had disappeared into the dining room. She had no time for chit chat.

Bryn, sitting at the head of the table in the dining room, was overwhelmed with the proceedings, especially as there were a number of people from the local chapel present as well, including the Revd. Isaac Howells who led the services in Horeb once a month, Frank Leyshon who was the organist there, Mr. Haydn Macdonald and his wife Susie and Miss Dorothy Roberts and her sister Marjorie. He spoke amicably to all who shared his table. 'Here's to you Lillian Shanks,' he said quietly to himself as he nodded his head and raised to shoulder level, his glass of mineral water.

When it was time for the coffee to be served he excused himself from the table and went to speak to each and every person who had come to support the event. He was delighted to see Mrs. Webb, Mrs. Pierce, Mark Mason and Miss Gwen Nelson who lived in the Waun Wen Sheltered Housing complex. Ken Thomas had kindly given them a lift.

'We won't be able to come next week, Vicar.' said Mark. 'We're off on a day trip to St Deiniol's.'

'We'd like to come again though if Ken will be willing to give us a lift. It's been really lovely. Thank you very much.'

Bryn then took a stroll outside to speak to the people who had preferred to eat in the open air. Four young women were sitting around a table on the patio. He recognised Sharon Morgan and Amy John; he had baptised their children at the same service some years before, but he didn't know the others.

'Hello Vicar,' said Amy. 'that was a beautiful lunch. By the way, these are my friends Felicity and Lynwen. You know Sharon already.'

'It's good to see you here ladies, and I hope that you will be able to join us on another occasion.'

'We've already asked for tickets for the Buffet and we'll be bringing our children with us to that,' said Amy.

'And we'll all come to church first,' stated Sharon. 'I hope it doesn't cave in! I've got to be honest, I haven't set a foot inside since the Christening, but I'm going to start coming again. My mother told me that, when I was a child, she had to cancel a holiday on one occasion because the dates were from a Sunday to a Sunday and I would not, on any account, miss Sunday School. Do you still have a Sunday School at St. Mary Magdalene?'

'Indeed we do,' Bryn replied, 'and a very thriving one at that. We are so fortunate to have such dedicated and able teachers and I'm proud to report that the children play an active part in our parish life.'

'Do you think my kids would fit in?' asked Sharon. 'The girls know how to behave, but Rhydian is plain mad.'

'Suffer the little children.........' replied Bryn.

He could sense a need here. Maybe attendance at a few services would do the trick. Bryn left the group to enjoy their time together. Lillian's effort at outreach had been realised.

Many parishioners remained behind to help clear up and by 3:00p.m. everything had been cleared away and the vicarage had assumed normality once more.

A rare smile appeared on the face of Mrs. Lillian Shanks. Helen believed that she was feeling a sense of achievement at a job well done. Smiles from Lillian seemed to be unusually few and far between. Tom Matthews appeared from the study. 'We've made £196.50p including donations, and Huw is still counting the monies taken for the raffle.'

'I'm on my way,' said Huw as he came in to the kitchen. 'The raffle has raised £57.'

'What a creditable achievement!' exclaimed Bryn. 'Thank you ladies for all your hard work, and special thanks *must* go to Mrs. Lillian Shanks.'

'I'm glad it all went so well Vicar. I hope that the men will be equally successful with their ham salads in two weeks time. Thank you and goodbye.'

After they had bidden farewell to the remainder of the group Bryn and Jennie stood in the porch in silence, gazing at the beautiful flowers that were blooming in the garden. If this, the first of the Midsummer Lunches, was anything to go by, then this year's fund raising event was sure to be a resounding success.

The weather on 21st June was cloudy but dry. Jennie had set the tables in exactly the same manner as for the previous lunch. She was on her way back to the kitchen when she glanced out of the window. Staggering up the path, reeling and swaying as though completely intoxicated, was the church treasurer, Mr. Tom Matthews. Jennie hurried to the window to take a closer look and discovered that his unusual gait was due to the fact that this feeble, elderly gentleman was carrying far too much at one time. He must have been carrying twelve pounds of potatoes at the very least, with a plate of best York ham that was gently slipping from its grip, which was just below his chin.

'*Do come in*,' Jennie called to Tom as she hurried to meet him.

She caught the plate of best York ham just as it began to make a downward plunge. Tom placed the bags of potatoes on the worktop, took out his handkerchief, gasped and mopped his brow. 'Good thing the church money bags aren't as heavy as this, or I'd never make it to the bank. There must be enough potatoes there to feed a regiment. I suggest that we boil them the in their skins.'

The doorbell rang again.

'Come straight in, we're in the kitchen,' called Jennie.

It was Phil Pugh. '*Me and my sa-a -a-lads!*' he sang cheerily. 'Shall I put them on the kitchen table? There are a few more bowls in the car. I'll fetch them now.'

As Jennie was carrying the bowls into the dining room she noticed, through the cling-film, that most of the eggs had black rings around the yolk. She wondered if Mrs. Lillian Shanks would be equally observant. As she was walking back into the kitchen she saw Charles Harris by the open door.

'*Do come in* Charles. We're in the kitchen.'

'*Ooooo* am I feeling fruity!' he said, looking at Jennie and shaking his body suggestively. '*Tutti-frutti* as we used to say years ago.' Charles was responsible for the fresh fruit salad. He moved closer towards her and whispered in her ear, 'Do you prefer a *kiwi* or a *pee-wee* Mrs. Vicar?' Jennie made no reply so after a short pause he went on to say, 'Would you like to have a little meander with me down the path and give me your hand…er….I .mean give me *a* hand?'

Charles Harris considered himself to be a real Casanova. Jennie accompanied him, in silence, to the parked car. She was very fond of Charles and respected his vast knowledge of the animal kingdom and his gardening expertise but at times like this she found him rather irritating and offensive. He opened the car boot to take out the two remaining fruit salad bowls.

'Would you carry this bowl please Jennie?' he asked. 'It's got cashew nuts and pecans in it, so I hope that nobody has a nut allergy. However, it's a perfect presentation although I say it myself.'

The car boot closed with a loud thud and they both made their way back to the house.

'I think we'll put the fruit salads on the dresser in the dining room Charles,' said Jennie as they got to the front door.

'*Fresh*,' replied Charles with a wink and a nod. 'These are no ordinary fruit salads, they are *fresh, fresh, fresh*' emphasising the words as though to imply a particular meaning.

Jennie went on to recite the first two verses of Psalm 57 quietly in her mind and wondered again why God had not allowed the life of the church hall cooker to be extended over the period of the Midsummer Lunches.

By 12:45 the Men's Society Ham Salad Lunch was in full swing and every seat had been taken, both inside the house and elsewhere on the premises. The three Roman Catholic priests from the nearby presbytery were present - Father Mark, Father Michael and Father Dewi.

'Their housekeeper must have the day off,' Charles was heard to say in the kitchen.

Mr. Haydn Macdonald and his wife were present again and Bryn was delighted that the event was becoming an ecumenical affair, especially as all people share a common destiny! Also present was a group from the local branch of Teimlo, which encompassed people with mental health problems, and the guffaws and laughter that were coming from their direction signified that they were having a good time. They attended St. Mary Magdalene as a group at Christmas, Easter, Pentecost, Harvest and Remembrance Sunday and Bryn led a monthly service in their residence so, over the years, he had got to know them very well as individuals. They regarded Bryn as one of their closest friends. He had been invited to their annual art displays and coffee mornings and other events that were held during the year. He maintained that the art work and simple sculptures conveyed messages and thoughts more significantly than a thousand spoken words could ever do.

Mrs. Lillian Shanks kept a low profile on this occasion. She had one very successful Midsummer Lunch under her belt and she would soon need to focus on her next enterprise. There was no way that she was going to interfere with the Men's Society's effort. As she was leaving she walked across to Tom Matthews who was standing by the door.

'I've enjoyed my lunch very much. Thank you. I hope that it has been a financial success also. Goodbye.'

He had counted up over £205 including the raffle, but an additional £15 was made at the very end of the proceedings when Charles's well presented yet untouched to the point of being surplus, *fresh* fruit salad was auctioned. Jennie did not bid. In fact, the salad in question went to the presbytery.

The third of the lunches was organised by The Flower Guild, under the strict jurisdiction of Mrs. Lillian Shanks. The weather on Friday 6th July was less kind than on the two previous occasions. There was a nasty drizzle and a cool south-easterly wind, so it was impossible to use the great outdoors.

May and Helen had prepared the melon balls at home along with a tuna bake and the 'throw it all in' pasta that Helen called her very own *creation*. It included olives, pickled onions, sliced beetroot and anchovies and, according to Helen, it enhanced the activity of the brain. She was supposedly speaking from experience. Mrs. Martha Jones supplied an enormous saucepan of spaghetti bolognaise and Mrs. Margaret Jones had made a selection of rice dishes.

The cheese and biscuits were donated by Mrs. Ida Phillips and Mrs. Phyllis Rees. Because most of the preparation was to be done in their own homes the working party, as they called themselves on this occasion, arranged to come to the vicarage at about mid-day. At twelve o' clock precisely the door bell rang. It was Lillian Shanks.

'A nice day for ducks but not a nice day for a function,' was her opening remark. 'Is there no-one here yet? We still have a lot to do my dear.'

Just as she had finished speaking Jennie could see May and Helen walking towards the door.

'*Do come in*,' called Jennie.

Helen put her heavy bags of goodies on the worktop and paused to catch her breath.

Lillian looked across the kitchen.

'Oh dear! I *do* hope that there will be enough to go around. Is that May's contribution as well or is it just your own? And I thought you promised melon balls Helen dear. They're not tucked up in those bags surely?'

'Mum is carrying the melon balls in as we speak, and without further ado I shall return to the car to fetch the rest of our contributions.'

As she walked out of the kitchen with her back towards Lillian she pulled a grotesque face and appeared to be doing some finger exercises on both hands. Soon Helen returned to the kitchen, accompanied by an empty-handed Martha. This was noted immediately by Mrs. Shanks.

'We need donations as well as delegates Martha dear. Did you not bring anything along?'

'It's in the car Mrs. Shanks. The saucepan is much too heavy for me to carry. Is the Vicar around to help me please Jennie? I think it will be too heavy even for you.'

'I'll fetch it,' said Helen, jumping at the chance to display her physical prowess in front of Mrs. Lillian Shanks. She bared her teeth and raised her arms as she attempted to show off her muscles. She discovered that she was able to carry the saucepan with no difficulty whatsoever, and with a wry smile placed it on the cooker. She returned to the car to collect the floral table decorations.

The first twenty five people to arrive were able to sit at table, either in the dining room, in the kitchen or in the living room where a picnic table had been erected. Others sat where they could find a space rather than a place. It was necessary for everybody to be accommodated indoors on this occasion. Some of the men sat on the stairs, while others stood in the kitchen, remaining mindful, not so much of the needs of others as had been mentioned in the pre-lunch prayer, but of the needs of Mrs. Lillian Shanks as she controlled and patrolled this particular area.

Despite the weather conditions however, yet again the event proved to be a resounding success and Tom Matthews was able to announce that the monies raised on this, the third Midsummer Lunch, was likely to be in excess of £250. Everybody was delighted with the result, especially Mrs. Shanks.

As the working party was making its way to the front door, she shouted, '*Stop!!* One moment please! We catered well. No waste. Thank you all very much indeed.'

In seemingly no time at all the day of the '*Buffet Magnifique*' arrived. No places were set for this meal, but there was plenty of seating available, either in the kitchen, the dining room, the lounge, or Bryn's study, and Jennie had made the upstairs television room accessible for the children, where they could watch a DVD or generally hang out.

Jennie expected more people to come to this event than the others, although those, too, had been very well supported. She had observed over the years, that when an event is held immediately following a church service almost 100% of the congregation participates. The event didn't coincide with a bowls match, a retired teachers' dinner, a senior citizens meeting with guest speaker or a WI choir practice. The minister from Horeb had purchased a dozen tickets and the Presbytery had bought four, so either the Roman Catholic Bishop would accompany the three Fathers or the ticket was for their housekeeper. It was highly unlikely that one of them would be bringing a girl-friend along; moreover it was quite out of order for one to speculate!

Sunday 22nd of July turned out to be one of the hottest days of the year. Jennie was up shortly after six o'clock and began to place the drinks and glasses on the kitchen table, from where they would be served. She was calling it 'the bar' for the coming hours. There were several boxes of Australian red wine, at least ten bottles of Californian white in the refrigerator, and six bottles of Rose. There was also plenty of fruit juice, mineral water and soft drinks for those who did not want to imbibe. Most of the drinks had been donated by a parishioner who wanted to remain anonymous. On the other hand, Charles Harris incessantly referred to his successful visit to the French hypermarket!

Jennie quickly showered and started on her tasks. She removed two large casserole dishes of Beef bourguignon from the fridge and a large pot of Chicken Chasseur, and placed them in the rayburn to reheat slowly. She then carved an enormous piece of beef. .. (Her butcher must have been laughing all the way to the bank. Either that or he could afford to take the following day off!). By 8:30 a.m. Jennie was ready for the onslaught.

Everything was in place, even down to the last plastic beaker for the children. Not too long afterwards there was a ring at the doorbell.

'*Do come in*,' called Jennie.

It was Lillian Shanks bringing her contribution. It was a whole salmon.

'Thank you very much indeed,' said Jennie. 'That looks most professional.'

'You're welcome Jennie.'

She took a step closer and lowered her voice, although there was no-one else around at the time.

'Jennie my dear, would you ensure that nothing sub-standard is placed on the table today. We don't want to lower the tone. You know what to look out for don't you? I know I've mentioned this before. Thank you. I'll see you later.'

Jennie seemed to spend the rest of the morning prior to the Eucharist calling, *'Do come in!!!'* She hoped that her voice would hold out for the rendition of the Welsh hymn *'Dyma Gariad fel y Moroedd'* that she was due to sing with Lucy before Bryn read the Gospel prior to delivering his sermon.

May came in bearing a large tray of cooked meats. It was, indeed beautifully presented as was Helen's lemon cheesecake. Ida placed her plate of assorted sandwiches on the table and Pat apologised for the quiche that she had left far too long in the oven. Phil and Chris Pugh proudly presented their salad bowls.

'Is there any way that we can prevent these black rings appearing on the boiled eggs?' asked Phil. 'It happens every time.'

At that moment Thelma arrived with her contribution. 'It's Sod's law! These queen cakes have turned out just like rock cakes. I didn't have time to bake a second batch. Never mind, they all go in the same way and come ….. well, I won't say anymore!'

By the time Jennie was ready to leave for the service the table was groaning and many other contributions were displayed on the dresser. This *Buffet Magnifique* was truly magnificent and included a variety of cold meats, casseroles, fish dishes, rice dishes, vegetarian dishes and much, much more. There was only sufficient space left on the dining table to put a decimal point! The parishioners of St. Mary Magdalene had, yet again, been extremely generous and supportive. Jennie felt that it was a privilege to be part of this wonderful parish. She hoped that God wasn't going to suddenly uproot them.

The church was full for the Eucharist that Sunday morning. In fact, Huw and Meirion had carried a dozen chairs from the church hall and had placed them strategically in the aisle, where they would not be part and parcel of a health and safety issue. Bryn delivered a most inspiring sermon, based on Isaiah's, 'Here am I! Send me!' and the duet given by Lucy and Jennie had been sung with emotion and sincerity, paving the way for what Jennie regarded as one of Bryn's best sermons of all time.

After the service people began to make their way over to the vicarage for the last of the Midsummer Lunches. Lillian Shanks and Jennie had left during the singing of the last hymn, to make sure that everything would be ready on time. Jennie turned up the heat under the potatoes that had already been boiled by Charles Harris. She was most grateful that there had been neither tutti- fruittis, kiwis or the preferred alternative included in his contribution this time.

About seventy adults supported the lunch and between twenty five and thirty children, most of whom either disappeared upstairs to the television room or went outside to play in the garden. Jan Bevan managed to sell three complete books of raffle tickets and almost half of the one that Beryl Francis had conveniently put in her handbag, just incase it was required.

By about mid- afternoon most people were beginning to leave. Charles Harris, however, had found a new lease of life and went into the kitchen with the intention of refilling his wine glass for the *nth* time. Bryn was looking out of the kitchen window in deep meditation.

'*Hoi! Barman!* I didn't hear you calling last orders. I'll have a large glass of red if you please.'

'There is no more wine,' replied Bryn, either intentionally or unintentionally, making this familiar Biblical reference.

'I've heard that somewhere before and I know what happened next too! Come on Vicar, have a go! *You can do it!* It was only plonk I brought back from France, now we can enjoy the good stuff. I'll fill this jug with water and you can see what you can do. I won't tell a soul. *I promise!'* Charles was becoming increasingly excitable. 'Go on Vicar, have a go! *Please!* Your line manager is very understanding so we're led to believe. Are you up for it?'

Bryn felt that the situation was getting just a little out of hand and was overjoyed when Charles settled for a substantial glass of malt whisky instead. Meanwhile, Tom Matthews was in the study counting up the takings. An announcement was due within the next five minutes.

All the children had left, so Jennie made a quick visit to the television room to survey what she expected to be a disaster zone. She couldn't believe her eyes. Everything was in its place, and the television had even been switched off at the mains in order to save energy. These kids were welcome anytime! As she hurried back downstairs she saw that Lillian Shanks was just about to leave. 'Thank you for everything Lillian. These Midsummer Lunches have been a huge success.'

'Tell me about it!' she replied with an air of superiority. 'And today's event alone has passed the £650 mark, or so I've been told by our treasurer. I understand that our 'andsome bishop made a creditable contribution in his absence. Thank you and goodbye.'

Bryn and Jennie retired early that night. They were both exhausted after experiencing the four weeks of intense entertaining along with the general day to day activities of parish life, the meetings at the vicarage, the social events and the spiritual opportunities that they felt they should support. However, everything had gone superbly and, as Lillian Shanks had predicted, the parish had reached out to the wider community.

As Bryn laid his head on the pillow that night, he raised his right hand heavenwards and said audibly, 'Lillian Shanks….. to you be the glory, great things you have done!' and with that he fell fast asleep.

PART 3:
2004→

Chapter 6: THE PARISH PILGRIMAGE

RIO BUM

The parishioners of St. Mary Magdalene, Rhydbrychan always enjoyed the annual church outing. Bryn had arranged several very interesting visits since the inaugural pilgrimage to the Shrine of Our Lady at Penrhys some years earlier, when all participants seemed to experience a sense of spirituality that they had never encountered before. The following year Bryn had organised a visit to some very old churches in the Hafod Deanery in the Diocese of St. Deiniol's. He had arranged for the incumbents of these parishes to speak to the group and bring to notice anything of theological or historical interest.

Everyone seemed refreshed by the visit and Bryn had been requested to arrange a similar excursion the following year. On this occasion they went to the Mynydd Mawr Deanery, and arrangements had been made for the bell-ringers of St. Mary Magdalene to ring a peal at the church of Holy Trinity, Aber Alun. During his introductory address The Revd. Robert Howe had eulogised over the magnificent bells that hung in the belfry, and had explained in detail the manner of their restoration. He described to the visitors the various fund-raising events that had taken place over a four year period, and read out a list of donations received during that time.

The recent grant from the Representative Body of the Church in Wales meant that overheads had now been brought to a bare minimum, and he hoped that all expenses regarding the restoration would be paid off by the end of the next financial year. Eventually the bell ringers were able to embark on their long but successful peal of bells in that place.

Unfortunately, Father Howe had forgotten to mention this event during the announcements on the previous Sunday, so there was nobody at the church, apart from himself, to welcome the enthusiastic group. However, the sound of the bells ringing out over the village called many people to the church during the course of the afternoon, and some of the members of the Mothers' Union even managed to provide the party with light refreshments, including home made scones and teisen lap.

On another occasion the parishioners had made a visit to St. Deiniol's Cathedral and Bryn had arranged for the Dean at the time, the Very Reverend Ivor Beer, to officiate at their midday service. Once again everyone seemed to enjoy the day out. On the way home in the coach Bryn had been asked repeatedly if another parish outing would be arranged for the following summer.

'God willing,' he replied, 'God willing.'

Quite clearly God was willing, because the next parish outing turned out to be the most successful to date. On that occasion it was held on a Sunday, beginning with a Eucharist in the parish church of St. Mary Magdalene. After the service fifty-three parishioners boarded the fifty-three seater Christiensen coach driven by Islwyn Isaac, who was also affectionately known as *'Aye! Aye!'* and set off to Neuadd Wen Country Park for a shared picnic lunch. Despite the fact that Father Jeffrey had omitted a supplication for good weather during the intercessions, it was a glorious day with temperatures reaching seventy five degrees or perhaps even a little more.

After lunch Meirion organised a game of baseball for the older children, whilst the younger ones had fun in the Adventure Playground. Many members of the group took a stroll in the gardens and some took a guided tour of the stately home. Suffice to say that each and every person, young or not so young, had a good time. At about five o' clock people began to gather their belongings together and returned to the coach for the next stage of the day's excursion.

From Neuadd Wen they travelled to Gaer Gelli where Bryn had served his title many years before. Representatives from both the parish of St. Cattwg, Gaer Gelli and the parish of St. Mary Magdalene, Rhydbrychan participated in the service. Mrs. Lillian Shanks had prepared her Old Testament reading well and delivered a dramatic account of 'The Crossing of the Red Sea' (Exodus 14 verses 15 -end). Lucy led the congregation in a few Taize chants, and Mr. Tom Matthews, licensed Reader of St. Mary Magdalene, offered the prayers. The hymns and responses were led by the choir of St. Cattwg's who gave a spectacular rendering of "Joy is like the Sun" - words by Martha Bowen and music by Josephine Dalkins.

It was the first time that any of those present had heard the aria and everybody was very impressed indeed. Bryn intended making enquiries regarding a CD recording and Pat, being so inspired with the rendering, was hoping to have a copy of the sheet music, if not there and then, as soon as possible thereafter. The sermon was delivered by the Reverend Sam Walters who was the present incumbent of St.

Cattwg's and also a close friend of Bryn. They had studied together at theological college many years before and had remained friends ever since.

Sam was far more active in the pulpit than Bryn ever was. During his twenty minute address he pointed upwards to heaven on numerous occasions, almost did a forward roll and a backward leap and, at one time, stamped his foot and simultaneously slapped his hand on the pulpit, to endorse a point. He even raised his voice and shook his fist, thus displaying behaviour that Bryn would never employ when giving a sermon. Jennie was amazed that the New Testament text chosen for Evensong - the compassionate miracle regarding blind Bartimaeus - could conjure up such a grand theatrical performance. Surely Jesus didn't bellow in a loud harsh voice, *'Recive your sight! Your faith has healed you!'* and go on to slap him on the head as Sam's gestures seemed to imply. Bryn always managed to express God's love for his world and for his people in a much calmer manner. At the end of the service everybody made their way into the church hall for what is fondly regarded in Ecclesiastical circles as a *'Bun Fight!'*

Clearly the people of St. Cattwg's had made a concerted effort with the catering arrangements. The display of food and fayre was comparable to that of a Wedding Reception, but without the balloons, favours and assigned seating. There was even a cake! It had been kindly donated by Arthur Price who owned 'Bara Beunyddịol,' the local bakery, and who was also the organist at St. Cattwg's Church. Modern technology had enabled a photograph of the church to be copied on the top of the cake with the words 'Welcome/Croeso' written in red icing on what one assumed to be the west door of the building. The group from St. Mary

Magdalene felt very much at home in such convivial company. People were chatting and laughing - some more raucously than others perhaps - as if they were members of 'Friends Reunited' or kept in touch on 'Facebook'.

At the end of the evening votes of thanks were given by Mr. Meirion Lloyd and Mrs. Hilda Grey. Martin Jones, the People's Warden at St. Cattwg's, promised to arrange a return visit ASAP! The Reverend Sam Walters said that he would like to give a blessing before the guests made their way back to the coach. There was complete silence as everyone bowed their heads, including the children, all of whom knew what was right and proper in such circumstances.

'Excuse me. Just one moment please,' said Lillian Shanks unexpectedly. Everyone raised their heads in a similar motion to that of a Mexican Wave.

'Before you start, Father, may I say a word?' she asked.

Everyone remained silent. There was obviously a Lillian sound-alike whom Sam had encountered during his ministry because he didn't seem in the slightest perturbed. Many clergy would have followed this simple request with unnecessary questions and chit-chat. Others might well have ignored her and merely carried on regardless. Not only did Sam have good manners; he was also able to empathise with all those with whom he came into contact.

'By all means. Of course,' the Reverend Sam Walters replied.

'The votes of thanks have been said, and I echo them whole-heartedly. However, what I would like to say is this. What we have experienced today must be similar to what pilgrims enjoy on a pilgrimage, not that I have ever been on a pilgrimage myself. Sadly I have never had the opportunity. However, during the service and here in this place, we have been spiritually uplifted. I am sure that I am speaking on behalf of everyone present. And I am certain that throughout the day we, as members of the parish of St. Mary Magdalene, have felt that sense of belonging, being a part of a family as it were. We leave this place with sound minds and grateful hearts. Thank you to all concerned. That is all.'

'Thank you for that Mrs. Shanks,' said Bryn, knowing that Sam would not have known the name of the person who had made these comments. There was a slight pause.

'And now the blessing,' said Sam as everybody bowed their heads for a second time. 'May the blessing of God Almighty, the Father, the Son, and the Holy Spirit be with you all, and all those whom you love, this night and for evermore. Amen.'

'***Amen***,' was the ardent reply from all those present.

People remained silent for a moment or two as they reflected on the events of the day, and what they had meant to them individually as Christians. Slowly folk began to move, and much jostling and cajoling followed as the parishioners of St. Mary Magdalene said their farewells to the people of St. Cattwg's and made their way to the church car park where their coach was waiting to take them home. The Reverend Sam Walters, surrounded by a crowd of his parishioners, came to bid the visitors farewell. A wonderful time had been had by all.

When everybody had boarded the coach, Islwyn offered them something that he thought they could never refuse.

'Hi there maties!' he shouted into his microphone as he threw his cigarette stub into St. Cattwg's car park. 'What grabs you for your on board entertainment? You can either listen to a CD of the best of Tom or I can put on a DVD. There's quite a choice here. I've got 'Hannibal' or 'The Silence of the Lambs' or there's 'The Sound of Music' if you want to sing along. Ain't got nothing specifically for kids though.'

Bryn explained that most of the children wanted nothing other than to sleep. They had had a fun packed day. He thanked Islwyn for the vast choice of entertainment, then asked the parishioners to indicate their preference for what was on offer by giving a show of hands. The silence that followed was comparable to that experienced by examination candidates reading a question paper that bore no reference to their course of study. Lillian was the first to speak.

'I propose that we all remain quiet and meditate on what we have experienced during the course of the day,' she suggested. 'Such spiritual opportunities are few and far between. We all need time to reflect.'

'I'll second that,' said Charles Harris. 'All I want to do now, is mull over what has been said and done today. I don't feel the need for Tom to tell me that I can keep my hat on, or to hear about the boy from nowhere, or even learn more about the sex bomb, strange as that may seem to you all! I really feel that we have all been somewhere today and no-one can take that from us. On this occasion it's thanks, but no thanks Islwyn.'

The passengers made the return journey in complete silence.

The coach pulled into the car park at St. Mary Magdalene's church at around 10:30 p.m.

'Thank you Vicar. That was lovely,' said Pat as she alighted from the coach. 'And you asked me to remind you about sending off for the sheet music.'

'I'll see to it first thing in the morning, Pat. Goodnight.'

'This has been the best parish trip so far,' said Huw Martin. 'A difficult one to follow. You'll have to put on your thinking skull cap if you see what I mean.'

'I'm glad you enjoyed. It was indeed a pleasant day,' replied Bryn.

'Those Taize chants went much better than I expected,' said Lucy as she jumped off the bus from the top step. 'We'll have to do them again some time. Goodnight Bryn and thank you.'

The last person to get off the coach was Mrs. Lillian Shanks. She had been checking that no personal belongings had been left behind. She did, however, find an umbrella. She handed it to Bryn. 'Does this belong to anyone in our party?' she enquired.

'Quite possibly,' he replied. 'I'll make an announcement on Sunday morning. If nobody claims it I'll drop it in at the depot when I'm passing. Is that alright with you, Islwyn?'

'Wassat? he asked. He was trying to light a cigarette with a dud match. 'Hold on Vic, just a mo!'

After he had successfully lit his cigarette he inhaled deeply and asked Bryn to repeat what he had said. Bryn explained about the lost umbrella.

'Well, it ain't mine, Vic, that's for sure. I'd look like a real ponce carrying that pink parasol. It would break my mother's heart. Anyway, I'm off now, Vic. See you again.'

'Thank you very much, Islwyn. Bye for now,' said Bryn.

With that, Islwyn revved up with a roar and drove away. He had almost completed his shift. *'Hoi! You up there!'* he called, glancing upwards as he drove into the bus garage. 'Thanks for helping me to keep them folks safe. By damn, when it comes to *PA*s you must be number one!'

The following day Bryn discovered that the umbrella belonged to Martha, Cwmdu.

'Thank you Vicar for a memorable day,' Mrs. Shanks had said as Christiensen Coaches had pulled off. 'It was full of fun, friendship and fellowship - the main ingredients of a pilgrimage or so I am told. May I thank you here privately Vicar, for what has been, for me, a day that I will never forget either socially or spiritually. Thank you and goodnight.'

With that she walked quickly away, indicating that their conversation was over.

One Sunday a few weeks later Bryn noticed that he had only one announcement regarding events for the coming week. The monthly meeting of the Mothers' Union was to be held in the church hall on Monday at 7:30 p.m. and the speaker was to be Mrs. Angela Murphy, wife of the Venerable Patrick Murphy, the recently appointed Archdeacon of Caergwenallt.

She would be talking about her work amongst children with learning difficulties; she and Jennie had been colleagues for a short time some years before. Apart from that it seemed to be a quiet week in the parish so Bryn thought that this might be an opportune moment to arrange a meeting regarding the possibility of a residential pilgrimage.

'I'm sure that you all remember the successful parish outing we had recently,' he announced from his reading desk that Sunday. 'It seems that it was enjoyed by all.' He paused, 'I am already thinking about next year, and I am wondering if any of you would be interested in being part of a group to make a parish pilgrimage to The Shrine of Our Lady in Walsingham in Norfolk. This could take place over a weekend or even over a few days in the week, depending of course on accommodation availability at the Shrine. There will be a meeting for anyone who may be interested in the Vicarage on Friday at 7:30 p.m. when I will explain more fully what the pilgrimage will entail. Thank you. There are no further announcements so……..Let us pray.'

'Shall I put out a few extra chairs in the sitting room?' asked Jennie, shortly before Friday's meeting was due to begin.

'If you bring two in from the dining room, I think that will be more than enough,' replied Bryn. 'I'm not really expecting many.' He paused. 'If any,' he added despondently.

At 7:25pm the doorbell rang.

'I'll get it,' said Jennie as she walked to the door. It was Mrs. Lillian Shanks. *'Do come in'* she said as she escorted Mrs. Shanks into the sitting room. 'Take a pew. I'll be back now. I'll leave the front door ajar so that people may simply walk in.'

On her way back to the sitting room she made a brief detour via the kitchen, where Bryn was attempting to complete the daily crossword before the meeting began.

'You'll *never* guess who's turned up,' she whispered. 'It's Lillian Shanks. What a surprise! You could have knocked me down with a feather!'

'I'm not surprised Jen. I'm not surprised at all,' replied Bryn with sincerity.

Jennie returned to the sitting room.

'Hello!' called Father Jeffrey from the doorway.

'Do come in,' said Jennie. 'We're in here.'

'I've brought Bob and Nancy with me,' he said as he walked in. Bob and Nancy Hughes had recently retired to Rhydbrychan from Allt-y-Groes where Bob had been the head-teacher of the local primary school. Since moving into the area they had attended services in a number of churches within the Deanery. However, they had soon found their niche in the parish church of St. Mary Magdalene. Not only had they found the parishioners particularly warm and welcoming, but they believed Bryn's sermons to be well prepared and informative. The added bonus of bells and smells on Saints Days was, if they needed one, the deciding factor.

By 7:35 p.m. on the evening of the pilgrimage meeting eight of the nine available chairs were occupied. Those present were Bryn and Jennie, of course, Mrs. Lillian Shanks, Father Jeffrey, Bob and Nancy Hughes, Huw Martin, and Mrs. Hilda Grey.

'I should imagine that everyone who wants to be here is here by now,' said Bryn, 'so shall we begin with prayer? We will be silent for a moment as we experience God's presence amongst us.' Everyone sat still.

'Yoo-hoo!' called a strident voice. 'The door was open so I walked straight in. Hope you don't mind,' he said, banging the front door behind him. It was Charles Harris. Speaking from the hallway he said, 'It's all very quiet here. Am I the first? Where are we Jen? In the den?' and he made his way into the sitting room. He noticed immediately that those gathered appeared to be in deep meditation. 'Sorry folks' he said, displaying some embarrassment and he sat in the remaining empty chair.

Bryn began to pray. 'Let us ask God's blessing on our meeting this evening. We ask that he will be with us to help us and to guide us and to show us the way.' He paused for a moment before offering prayers for the world at large, remembering especially those in need. The intercessions were brought to an end with everyone saying the Lord's Prayer together, followed by the Grace. Bryn welcomed everybody to the meeting and asked if any other parishioners had shown interest.

'Pat Lewis telephoned me from Devon this afternoon and said that she would like to be included,' he said.

Hilda Grey was the next one to speak. 'Lucy can't make it tonight. She's entertaining the St. Ann's branch of the Mothers' Union as part of the Llwynderw Fiftieth Anniversary celebrations.'

'Meirion told me that he was interested, but he's got a meeting at the Top Hat Club tonight,' said Huw. This was a club for businessmen and professionals. Moreover, it was a 'men only' club. Meirion's dedication and faithfulness to his parish church only marginally exceeded that of his dedication and faithfulness to his beloved *T.H.C.* as it was often called.

'There are nine present tonight, plus the three people who have been mentioned, so that means at least a dozen people are interested. There may be others of course. However, as we are all aware, twelve is a significant number and much can be experienced within a group of this size.' Bryn paused. 'I am sure that a residential Parish Pilgrimage can be of great significance in many ways. I first became a Walsingham Pilgrim when I was at Theological College. In fact, the Reverend Sam Walters was part of the group on that occasion. Jennie and I have attended the Annual Anglican Pilgrimage several times and I also took part in the Diocesan Pilgrimage a few years ago, when it was led by the notorious Bishop Johnny. Say no more! Anyway, Walsingham is a place to which one has the desire to return again and again. It is, as one may say, unique.'

He went on to explain how Walsingham had become a place of prayer and spirituality and that it was known all over Europe as England's Nazareth.

'Walsingham is in Norfolk, a very beautiful part of the country,' said Bryn.

'Excuse me Vicar,' said Bob Hughes, 'but I noticed in the prayers that you asked God to show us the way. Maybe you were thinking of something spiritual, but if not, Nancy and I have friends in Great Snoring, which is only a few miles away from the Shrine, so I know the way like the back of my hand.'

Bryn reflected for a moment and then he smiled. 'Thank you for that Mr. Hughes. That will be most helpful.'

He went on to outline a possible schedule which included

- A daily Eucharist service

- Visits to the Holy House

- Stations of the Cross

- Sprinkling at the Well

- Procession of Our Lady

- Hymns and Intercessions

'That's enough from me for the moment,' Bryn concluded. 'Are there any questions?'

'I have a question Vicar,' Lillian Shanks replied. 'Is there a pianist available?' Once again her Yorkshire lilt came to the fore. 'By that I mean will Pat be responsible for accompanying us on the piano? If so, I'm sure that she would like to practice the hymns well in advance.'

'A very good question, Mrs. Shanks. 'We will be depending on Pat for our group services but, when we join with other pilgrims for worship, then the Shrine Staff will make all the necessary arrangements.'

'Thank you Vicar. No further questions.'

It was decided that the Parish Pilgrimage would take place from Monday 21st July to Thursday 24th July of the following year. Bryn would make enquiries regarding mini-bus hire and accommodation availability at the Shrine. Full board was to be included. Bryn closed the meeting with The Blessing and all the would-be pilgrims left the vicarage 'on a high.' '*Who-oo* would true valour see, let him come hither,' sang Charles Harris as he skipped down the vicarage drive - and he continued to sing the whole verse.

Huw Martin soon caught up with him.

'An excellent meeting, eh?'

'I should say.' Charles paused for thought. '*What!*- me a pilgrim? My mother would be proud of me.' Charles Harris, at the age of seventy, had lost his mother many years before. Shortly before she had made the final crossing she stated quite clearly her belief in the words of a well-known hymn:

'O happy band of pilgrims

If onward ye will tread,

With Jesus as your fellow

To Jesus as your head.'

'Life is a pilgrimage my boy,' she went on to say. 'Hold on to your faith.' Mrs. Rosemary Harris had died peacefully in her sleep two days later.

The final meeting regarding the Parish Pilgrimage was held in the Vicarage on the last Friday in June of the following year. Jennie had made sure that there were thirteen seats available in the sitting room - twelve seats for the pilgrims and one for the Pilgrim Father. No other names had been submitted over the year. Although Chris Pugh had shown an interest in the trip, particularly in the full board arrangements, it transpired that the school term didn't finish until after the pilgrimage had taken place. Thelma had put her name down 'in pencil' as it were, but then discovered that the dates coincided with her annual visit to sunny Cala Bona in Spain.

'Pity, I could do with an uplift!' she had said to Charles Harris as he glanced at her cleavage after a Sunday Eucharist. 'The Vicar told me that the chances of that were very high.'

'Seeing is believing!' replied Charles with a snide grin.

Tom Matthews was almost devastated when he discovered that he couldn't join the group. He loved Walsingham and claimed that he had been there more times than he had changed his socks and, as he was a bachelor, this remark was somewhat feasible. However, his niece Rhianne was getting married in the Caribbean and he would be flying out to Kingston, Jamaica on the same day that the pilgrims would begin their pilgrimage.

'I don't mean to be blasphemous,' he had said to Bryn, 'but I think I'll be closer to God than you will be when we set off.' He pointed to the heavens. 'I'll have at least a thirty five thousand feet headstart.'

It was 6:50 p.m. when the doorbell rang. Jennie didn't expect a prospective pilgrim to arrive ten minutes ahead of time.

'It must be someone for you, Bryn,' she said. 'Banns of marriage, perhaps.'

'Can you answer it anyway please love? I just want to check something in this Walsingham folder.'

Jennie opened the door. It was Meirion Lloyd. 'Hello Meirion,' she said. *'Do come in.* We're meeting in the sitting room.'

'Hi Jennie. I've come early because I have to leave early. There's a very important meeting in the *THC* tonight and I feel that I should be there. I've come to pay my dues for the pilgrimage. How much per head is it? Bryn didn't say. I know it's said that two heads are better than one but am I glad I've only got one at this point. Do they do a *B.O.G.O.F.* in Walsingham? - you know what I mean, buy one get one free!'

'Just take a seat Meirion,' said Jennie somewhat weakly.

'Where shall I take it Jennie?'

Meirion was certainly on form. Just as Jennie was about to call Bryn he appeared in the doorway of the study.

'Meirion wants to pay up before he's up and off,' she said.

They each took a seat in the sitting room.

'You've got a bargain break here Meirion, that's for sure,' laughed Bryn. 'Four days away from home, three breakfasts, three lunches, three suppers, umpteen teas and/or coffees, entrance to Ely Cathedral, an afternoon excursion and over five hundred miles of travel; probably more like six hundred when you come to think of it, and all for a mere £160. What more could a man want?'

'A beautiful woman!' replied Meirion, which was rather strange as he was a committed dog lover.

Secretly he was dreading putting his four dogs into the kennels. It meant that it was not only for the duration of the pilgrimage, but for a day either side as well. They were all 'rescue' dogs as he put it. There was Sali the sheepdog that didn't make the grade as a 'rounder upper' and Snoop the terrier, who in the early days of being taken in had been terrified of everyone and everything. Now he had acquired a knack of terrifying everyone and everything, both man and beast alike. Sadie was an abandoned Labrador. Meirion had successfully taught her to fetch his slippers and give a paw. He maintained that she was the equivalent of an A* student. And then there was Elsa. Her behaviour was impeccable. She sat, stood, sang to the piano and 'played dead' on request. She was quite a performer and was the only one of the four, when out walking in Parc Dewi, to respond to 'heel'.

'Let me write out a cheque now. I'm sorry that I have to leave early,' he said, 'but, as I explained to Jennie, there's an important meeting in the *THC* tonight. We're discussing possible financial assistance to the local paraplegic games and I really want to use my vote.'

'I fully understand your commitment,' replied Bryn.

'No chance of bringing the dogs to Walsingham I suppose?' asked Meirion.

'I'm afraid not,' replied Bryn. 'Where do you plan to leave them?'

'Doggie's Paradise in Pont Gwallter. No restrictions. They can bark, sniffle, drink and piddle round the clock.'

'Take heart, Meirion, my friend,' said Bryn with empathy, 'for they, too, will be on a pilgrimage!'

As soon as Bryn had finished speaking the doorbell rang. It was Mrs. Lillian Shanks.

'*Do come in*. We're meeting in the sitting room as usual,' called Jennie as she and Bryn returned to the kitchen. Meirion remained seated.

'Good evening,' said Mrs. Shanks pleasantly. 'Are you ready for the pilgrimage?'

'Financially at least. I've just paid up. Bryn insists that it's a real bargain break.'

'Be that as it may,' she replied. 'I'm not looking for a bargain. I'm in search of spiritual refreshment and this pilgrimage sounds ideal to me. I hope to come back a different person.'

'I bet your bottom dollar you do,' Meirion thought to himself, but said nothing.

'I have a feeling, from what the Vicar has said, that this place will be calling me back again and again,' she continued.

'In all fairness Mrs. Shanks,' Meirion replied, 'you can't expect the Vicar to arrange something as big as this year after year. The organization of it all, even for us twelve disciples, is astronomical.'

'I heartily agree Meirion, but, should this place provide the spiritual experience for which I yearn and to which the Vicar has referred, then I will embark on the journey independently. We'll just see how it goes. There we are,' and she sat in silence, smiling benignly.

The doorbell rang again and Meirion and Lillian heard Jennie say '*Do come in.*'

'I bet if she had a penny for every time she said that she'd be one of the richest women in the UK,' said Meirion.

Just as he was about to elaborate on his observation, a host of - not angels - but prospective pilgrims - arrived. Almost everybody arrived at the same time. Pilgrims seemed to be grabbing seats as if they were playing a game of musical chairs. At this point Jennie returned to the meeting and she really felt like telling them that there were enough seats for one per head. On second thoughts, she decided that such an exercise would not be practical. There were enough seats per seat - but - by the time she had worked out this explanation, there were no buts -all had been parked. The Parish Pilgrims were:

- Reverend Bryn Jenkins (Parish Planner/Plotter/Organizer etc.)

- Mrs. Jennie Jenkins

- Father Jeffrey

- Mrs. Lillian Shanks

- Dr. Huw Martin

- Mr. Meirion Lloyd

- Mrs. Pat Lewis

- Mr. Charles Harris

- Mrs. Hilda Grey

- Mrs. Martha Jones

- Bob and Nancy Hughes

- Lucy

'Let us begin with prayer,' said Bryn as he placed his Walsingham folder on the coffee table to his right. After the prayers had been said Bryn opened the meeting.

'A very warm welcome to you all. We're here tonight to finalise arrangements for next week's pilgrimage. I can't believe how quickly it has come around. We will have a short service in the Lady Chapel here in the parish church before leaving. Jennie will drive the mini-bus, taking all the pilgrims other than Huw, who will travel with me. Vestments, hymn books, keyboard, Lucy's guitar etc. etc. will be taken by car, thus allowing ample space in the bus for luggage and personal belongings, together with some light refreshments. There will be a few empty seats, so some luggage and excess baggage can be placed there. We do not want anything in the aisles, especially as, in this day and age, things appertaining to health and safety seem to be of greater importance than The Ten Commandments.' He smiled at his mini-flock. 'I can assure you that we are all in for a wonderful experience,' he added. 'There is even a chance that we may come back as different people, so to speak. We will all, in our own way, experience the presence of God. We have so much to look forward to.'

'I can't wait,' said Lucy. 'It sounds brill.'

'Excuse me Vicar,' said Meirion 'I'll be off now,' and he quietly left the room for his *THC* meeting.

'I'll get to wear my cassock every day,' said Father Jeffrey. 'No need for clean clothes.' He happened to catch the eye of Mrs. Lillian Shanks, whose facial expression seemed to exhibit unbelief and disdain.

'Only joking. *Honest!*' said Father Jeffrey. Clearly, Mrs. Lillian Shanks was not amused.

'Do you want to hear the good news or the bad?' asked Bryn with a glint in his eye.

'Oh, the good news please,' was the reply, almost in unison.

'Well, all the arrangements have been finalised. Actual room allocation will be given on arrival, but I don't for-see any problems there. We will all be staying in Stella Maris at the shrine site itself. No-one will be given a room above the butcher's, the baker's or the candlestick maker's as has been known in the past! Now for the bad news. I know I gave an estimate of £140 but I'm afraid the final cost has risen to £160 per head. I'm sorry about that.'

'If I chop my head off can I go for free?' laughed Charles Harris as he removed a wad of notes from his wallet. Having withdrawn a month's pension that very day he felt somewhat affluent. Lucy handed over the cheque that had been signed by her mother. 'Mum said whatever the cost, it's worth every penny. She won't hear me strumming and crooning, as she puts it, for a whole week.'

'Her loss will be our gain,' said Lillian Shanks quite unexpectedly. Lucy having been under the assumption that Mrs. Shanks was not in favour of guitar music in church was very much encouraged by the comment.

There was much chatter and excitement during the 'pay up' period and Jennie felt as though she was a member of The Get-Along Gang, and that these pilgrims were well and truly 'one for all and all for one.' She, herself, was really looking forward to the pilgrimage, despite the fact that she would be taking on the role of a bus-driver. When all the business had been dealt with Bryn asked everyone to join hands and say the words of The Grace together. The meeting was now closed.

It was early in the morning of Monday 21st July that the pilgrims gathered in the Lady Chapel of St. Mary Magdalene for a Eucharist before embarking on their journey. Jennie had collected the fifteen seater minibus from Mansel's Rentals the day before and had filled it with diesel ready for the trip. Following the escorted scrutinised tour of the vehicle she was fully aware of the fact that there was not a single mark or scratch on the bodywork, and she intended to do her utmost to keep it that way. She was more than familiar with the kind of vehicle itself, having driven the school minibus over a period of twenty five years. She had parked the hired motor, registration - R 10 BUM - in the church car park overnight.

As she locked the doors she remembered the message from one of Bryn's recent sermons, when he had stressed that what was on the inside far outweighed what was seen to be on the outside. She hoped that this elderly vehicle would be capable of completing the course, that its innards were in as good a shape as the exterior. She thought that the number plate bore particular significance, and the expression 'God knows' brought a new meaning to her. Bryn had placed the vestments, keyboard, hymn books etc. in his car so that they would be ready to leave immediately after the service.

By 8 o' clock the following morning they were all set to depart. Bryn came on to the bus to check that everything was alright and that nobody had forgotten anything.

'We won't attempt to travel in convoy,' he said. 'Jennie has had instructions as to when and where we'll meet up later so, Onward Christian pilgrims. Bon Voyage!'

Jennie found the driving quite easy. The motorways were relatively quiet and the passengers bore no resemblance to the bus load of uncouth youths whom she had driven some years previously. There was no swearing or fighting or unnecessary changing of seats; no spitting or forced 'throwing up' to attract attention; all seemed quiet on the western front - although they were travelling north - and everybody seemed to be enjoying the journey in their own way. She knew that Charles Harris was referring periodically to his AA map, but he assured her that he was following the route as opposed to checking her motorway crossovers. Martha spoke from time to time, drawing everyone's attention to a rare breed of sheep or a remote farmhouse. Lucy seemed to be composing some music and Hilda Grey, who was sitting directly in front of her, could hear her occasionally humming quietly as if checking dominants or sub-dominants. Father Jeffrey, his eyes closed and his Pilgrim Manual clutched in his right hand, was either at prayer or at ease. Bob and Nancy, who were sitting up front with Jennie, congratulated her on her driving, and told her about their many visits to Great Snoring.

'Excuse me Jennie,' came a voice from the back some time later. It was Mrs. Lillian Shanks. 'It's five minutes to twelve. Are you going to pull over on to the hard shoulder for mid-day prayers? I don't need to remind you that we are on a pilgrimage and the importance of prayer is paramount.'

'If it's all the same with you Lillian, I'd like to press on.' She looked into the rear view mirror at her passengers. 'Listen up everybody,' she called, just as she had done in those golden days of school trips. 'Mrs. Shanks has suggested that I pull onto the hard shoulder for mid-day prayers. Unfortunately, I don't think that will be very practical, but perhaps we could have a few minutes silence for personal meditation.'

'It's not hands together and eyes closed for you mind Jennie!' laughed Charles Harris. 'You've got ten exceptional bums on board.'

He, too, had noticed the vehicle's number plate. People remained quiet for some time. In fact, surprisingly little was said thereafter until the bus drew up at the assigned rendezvous. After the pilgrims were duly fed and watered they continued on their journey. As they approached the A14 Jennie put on a CD of Worship Songs. The pilgrims participated well, and even attempted a four part harmony for the Blaenwern composition of 'Love Divine'. Jennie was pleased with the way things were going.

'Great Snoring one and a half miles to the right,' said Bob, much later in the afternoon. 'Not far to go now.'

Within fifteen minutes after that Jennie was pulling into the car park at Walsingham. Bryn and Huw had already started to unload the car.

'I'm glad that we decided not to bring the parish banner as well,' Bryn thought to himself. 'Just carry what you can manage for the moment Huw,' he called. 'We can come back for the rest later.' Jennie practically jumped out of the driver's seat. She was so pleased that the journey had been uneventful and that everyone had seemed to enjoy it. Together the pilgrims made the short walk from the car park to the shrine. All their belongings were left in the common room at Stella Maris while they went immediately to make their First Visit to the Holy House. This was customary procedure by all pilgrims. They entered through the Pilgrimage Entrance at the West end of the Shrine Church and gathered in front of the Altar of the Annunciation.

Father Jeffrey read from St. Luke's Gospel and prayers were said. They then moved to the Holy House whilst reciting Psalm 84. 'How lovely is your dwelling place, O Lord Almighty! My soul yearns, even faints for the courts of the Lord; my heart and my flesh cry out for the living God.' They recited the twelve verses. After that they returned to the common room to collect their luggage and make their way to their allocated rooms. Although Charles Harris was a little disappointed that there had been no administrative error to enable him to bed down with Lucy, he didn't show it.

'If we could all congregate here at seven o' clock this evening we can go into supper as a group,' said Bryn. 'See you later.'

Everyone was on time, so they made their way to the Refectory where some pilgrims were already queuing.

'My word!' exclaimed Lillian Shanks with surprise, 'I haven't queued up for my supper since I was at boarding school. I feel quite rejuvenated! Are all meals on a queue-up basis Vicar?'

'I'm afraid so Mrs. Shanks. I trust that it is not going to be a problem.'

'Not at all Vicar, not at all.' She noticed that there was a space near the hot-plate. 'Move along Vicar we're getting closer to the serving hatch.' Before long they were being served. *'Oh! Yes please!'* said Mrs. Shanks as she was offered a substantial portion of chicken casserole that was served with an equally substantial portion of seasonal vegetables.

The group spent the rest of the evening in the Hollybush Inn. There was much hilarity and even a little sharing of jokes.

'Have I ever told you the one about Bishop Johnny in the museum? asked Charles Harris. 'Now he was the bishop of *all* bishops if you ask me. Never a dull moment, a laugh a minute, and some of the jokes he could tell would make your hair stand on end!'

Huw noticed an expression of disgust appear on Lillian's face and quickly assured Charles that they *had* all heard it before. Discussion turned to the plans for the following day. When the bell signifying 'last orders' was rung Charles, Huw and Father Jeffrey surged toward the bar as if they had reached the finishing line in the London Marathon.

'I'll get these,' Charles said. 'Same again please barman.' He called over to Bryn. 'Another pint of Revd. Evans, Vicar? It's really smooth.'

'No more for me thank you Charles,' he replied.

'How about you Mrs. Shanks?' he asked out of politeness rather than expectation. 'One for the road?'

'Oh yes please Charles. I'll have a Jack Daniels if I may. On second thoughts would you make it a double; on the rocks if you please with plenty of ice. Thank you, that is most generous of you.'

By midnight however, all the Rhydbrychan pilgrims were fast asleep. Angels and archangels had probably observed the manner in which their heads had hit their pillows in the sleeping quarters of the Shrine. It was comparable to a 'strike' in a bowling alley. Prior to this Bryn had had a short de-briefing with God and Pat had practiced some hymns on an imaginary keyboard on top of the duvet. All were at peace with the world - and with God of course.

Tuesday's agenda began with a Eucharist in one of the side chapels in the Shrine Church. Pat was glad that she had managed to practice 'My Song is Love Unknown' on the duvet cover the night before, especially since it was in the key of E flat major. For some reason or another she invariably goofed up this particular hymn but, on this occasion, apart from the incidental backing rhythm that had been switched on in error -and which she managed to turn off quickly - things went well.

After breakfast the group met together to follow The Stations of the Cross in the Shrine gardens, led by Father Jeffrey. A follow-up discussion session was held in the common room immediately afterwards. Quite clearly, every pilgrim had been spiritually moved by the experience. Bryn was the first to speak.

'Thank you Father Jeffrey for leading us along the Via Dolorosa by means of such an authentic approach. I believe that I have really travelled the Way of the Cross this morning, and as a result I feel more personally responsible for the events of Good Friday than ever before.' He paused for a moment. 'Thank you also to Lucy. You sang each verse of the hymn with such sensitivity, that- yes - I'm sure that I was there when they crucified Our Lord.' He paused again. 'Does anyone else have something to share?' he asked.

'Vicar, can I say something please?' asked Martha.

This was quite out of character, since Martha's only contributions to discussions were those regarding rare breeds of sheep and farming, Mothers' Union teas and the church cleaning rota. For her to be the first parishioner to contribute in this way was as great an accomplishment as Neil Armstrong's foot on the moon.

'Yes, of course Martha. Go ahead,' said Bryn with encouragement.

'Well Vicar, everybody, it's like this.' She bowed her head and clasped her hands. 'It's like this,' she repeated as she raised her head to make eye contact with those present. She spoke slowly as she savoured the memory. 'I just didn't want to go from there. I didn't want to leave the tomb. Some people thought that it was all over when Jesus was laid in the tomb, and when I was a youngster I wondered myself. But today, Vicar, I was there in the tomb with Him, and feeling His presence there has given me a brand new start on my life's journey, although I'm seventy six. Will there be time for me to go back to the tomb tomorrow Vicar?'

Bryn paused before replying so that the other pilgrims could reflect on Martha's contribution.

'There will be some free time tomorrow Martha, so perhaps you would like to go then. We will always be able to make time for anything that anybody wants to do. We are here for each other.' Everyone sat in silence for a moment or two.

Charles Harris was the next person to speak. Surprisingly, there were no malicious remarks regarding Martha's contribution, neither were there any suggestive comments as to their being there for one another. Charles, for once, was certainly displaying his serious mode of behaviour.

'Vicar,' he said. 'I've heard these words during Holy Week for the best part of seventy years. 'Crucify Him! Crucify Him!' In fact I've said them myself at many a Good Friday service when the congregation has been invited to participate in the gospel narrative. Today the message actually hit home to me!' He paused. '*We* condemned Jesus to death. Much like what you've said over the years, Vicar, I suppose, but I never felt really responsible for the events of Good Friday until today. I always thought that it was someone else. I believe that I have a lot to answer for.'

'I think I know what you mean Charles,' said Lucy. 'I felt really guilty when Jesus was carrying His cross.'

People sat in silence for a moment or two and then Meirion spoke. 'I wish in a way that I had been Simon of Cyrene. At least I could have helped Him to carry it.'

'The worst part for me was the actual crucifixion scene,' said Jennie almost in tears. 'I'm sorry, but I can't say any more at the moment.'

'This is the first time that I can honestly say that I've felt different,' said Hilda Grey. 'I don't know what it is.' She paused. 'In retrospect I think, I do really, maybe for the first time in my life I have been spiritually uplifted.'

A long pause followed as the pilgrims thought about the journey they had taken and what had been said as a result. Just as Bryn was about to draw the session to a close Mrs. Lillian Shanks began to speak.

'I don't know where to begin really,' she said. 'The whole experience has been overwhelming and something that I will never, ever forget. The prayers and the reflections that followed each Station are simply beyond description. It was the Fourth Station that had the greatest affect on me, I believe. It was, you remember, 'Jesus meets His Mother,' and it has nothing to do with the fact that my own child died at birth, I promise you. I just feel for poor Mary. The joy of the Angel's message must have been turned to deepest agony as she watched her son staggering down the road.' She cleared her throat before continuing. 'I have to admit that I had never really considered the impact that must have had on Mary on that first Good Friday. How she must have suffered. That is all. Thank you for listening.'

For the first time in her life, Mrs. Lillian Shanks had felt able to share her closest and most personal experience with others. Nobody had ever heard about her still-born child until now. A prayerful and respectful pause followed. Quite clearly the Parish Pilgrimage was proving to be a gateway to increased spirituality and shared understanding.

'Let us pray,' said Bryn. 'We thank you God for the opportunity to follow the Way of the Cross today and for the time that we can spend alone with you in this peaceful place. Help us to grow closer together so that we may truly become one family in the name of Christ. We ask your blessing on our pilgrimage. Amen.'

'Amen!'

'At two o'clock this afternoon we will gather for Sprinkling at the Well', said Bryn. 'We will meet in the nave of the Shrine Church together with other pilgrims who may be present. See you later.' Until then, everyone was free to do their own thing in their own time.

By two o' clock the members of the group were gathered in the Shrine Church as requested. Charles had read a notice as he had passed the Well earlier on; it was promoting the afternoon service. It read 'Sprinkling Today….. 2.00 p.m.' In a way it reminded him of a notice that had been displayed daily in the local fish and chip shop in Lwff-y-dwlb, the seaside village where he had grown up. 'Frying Tonight ….6:00 p.m.' it had read. Charles suddenly realised that such a comparison was sacrilegious and hurried into the Holy House to make a quick confession.

All the Rhydbrychan pilgrims attended the service and managed to get down the steep steps to the Well. They received the water in three ways:

- A sip of water to drink

- The sign of the cross on the forehead

- Water poured over the hands

They then returned to their places for further prayers and anointing, during which Bryn played a vital role. He participated in the laying on of hands.

The remainder of the day was free. Some of the group took a train ride to Wells-next-the-Sea. Others walked to the Slipper Chapel, which was a significant part of the Roman Catholic Pilgrimage.

Pat took the opportunity to practice some music on the keyboard. Martha was delighted to have the opportunity to make another visit to the tomb, where she knelt alone in prayer for some time. She was glad that nobody invaded her privacy. Later she went for an afternoon nap and fell asleep thanking God for letting her watch over Jesus in the tomb. She told Him that if she hadn't felt so tired she would have stayed longer.

Lillian Shanks sat on a seat in the grounds and took in the ambience of the surroundings. She was content. She was at one with herself, with the world and with God. She was experiencing a feeling of calm and relief that she had never felt before.

In fact, all the pilgrims were enjoying a sense of peace and tranquillity. They were so very grateful that Bryn had brought them to this place at this time. They all felt safe in the palm of God's hand.

That evening the Hollybush did a roaring trade. All the Rhydbrychan pilgrims were present, along with a large group from a parish in the Ystrad Valley. Pat was asked to play the piano, but, as she didn't have any music with her at the time, she was unable to oblige. Lucy, however, ran back to the shrine to fetch her guitar, and a memorable evening was had by all. 'She'll be wearing the Archbishop of Canterbury's winceyette night-shirt when she comes!' - well, Lucy managed to fit in all the words to the music to endorse the fact, along with the Queen's comfy corset, the Venerable's voluminous vest and the Dean's dirty dog-collar. Charles's chorus rendering of 'I will if you will so will I!' was completely drowned by the shrieks of the 'Aye, aye yipees!' At the end of the song everyone clapped and cheered. Spirits, in more ways than one, were running high. A brief silence followed as people caught their breath after all the hilarity. It was broken by the voice of Mrs. Lillian Shanks.

'Excuse me Vicar. Since we're all in good mood I would like to engage you in a little guessing game.' She looked around the bar, smiled and nodded and invited pilgrims from all places to participate. 'We're all in this together,' she said. 'It shouldn't take too long.'

'By all means Mrs. Shanks,' he replied. 'This sounds very interesting.'

'I am thinking of a letter of the alphabet and a word starting with it that describes our time together. Hands up. No shouting out please.'

Hilda Grey was the first to respond. 'S – Spiritual,' she said.

'And so it is, very much so dear, but that is not the correct answer.'

Bob was the next person to offer a suggestion.

'T - Togetherness.'

'No.'

'D - Devotional,' suggested Lucy.

'That is an excellent suggestion, but again the answer is 'no'.'

'P- Peaceful,' offered a pilgrim from the Ystrad Valley.

'I must congratulate you on your choice of word. It is so appropriate, but your guess is wrong. Do try again if you wish.'

'B - Blessed,' said Bryn.

'And so we are! However Vicar, although I am sorry to say, that is incorrect.' She waited a moment or two but it seemed that there were no suggestions forthcoming. 'The letter I am thinking of is……. '*f*'.' She stood up, downed her drink, acknowledged Jack Daniels, slapped the table and wagged her finger knowingly.

'Oh *no!*' thought Charles. 'Her eyes are sparkling and she's a bit flushed, but I didn't think she'd go as far as this. She's going to ruin everything. It's been such a wonderful day for us all. We'll never experience anything like this again.'

All Jennie could think of was fat, fatter and fattest as she still felt quite bloated after her evening meal. As for Martha, she was thinking farms and farming, but, at this point, nobody felt sufficiently confident to actually make a contribution.

'I hope that I have your full attention,' she said as an enormous grin filled the whole of her face, the like of which had never been seen before.

At this point Charles felt that she was going to blow it. He cringed on his barstool and waited for the worst. He should never have agreed to buy her the third double Jack Daniels of the evening. 'I'm really surprised that not a single Christian pilgrim can come up with an *f* word,' she said innocently. 'Isn't it obvious? Anyway, the answer to my guessing game is…' There was a short pause, although it seemed like a lifetime to Charles. '***F***un, ***F***riendship and ***F***ellowship - the ingredients of a happy and successful pilgrimage, and with that I bid you all goodnight.'

She closed the door with a slam as she left the bar, only to reappear a few seconds later. 'Amen. Alleluia! We have been richly blessed!' she shouted from the doorway and the door closed behind her. She had left everybody speechless. Charles got up from his barstool and slowly walked outside to the courtyard for some fresh air. He was feeling completely and utterly ashamed of himself.

After the Eucharist the following morning the group visited nearby Thurston, where they enjoyed listening to an old concert hall organ being played. After that they had a tour around the immediate area, stopping off at the parish church before returning to the shrine, where the time was their own until the Evening Devotions.

The Evening Devotion was held in the chapel of St. Augustine. Bryn had prepared a simple but meaningful service that focused on The Litany of Our Lady of Walsingham, and on which he based his short address. Pat's accompaniment to 'Daily, daily sing to Mary' and 'O purest of Creatures' was perfect, and the pilgrims sang with both fervour and emotion. Lucy had composed a tune to the words of 'For Mary, Mother of our Lord' especially for this service, and everybody was touched by her presentation.

'She has a voice just like an angel,' thought Lillian Shanks, as she bowed her head in prayerful meditation.

Charles Harris was also thinking, albeit not quite so prayerfully, 'I wonder if she will be willing to come and do a gig for one of our rugby charities?' he thought. 'What with her figure and her voice we'd make a bomb.'

At the end of the hymn there was complete silence as everybody reflected on what had been sung. Father Jeffrey brought the devotions to an end with The Sub Tuum Praesidium, which is the Church's oldest prayer to Our Lady and was written after the Council of Ephesus in 431.

After supper all the Walsingham pilgrims met for the Procession of Our Lady and Benediction. The image of Mary was carried and everyone seemed to experience a sense of companionship and inter- dependency as they walked together through the beautiful grounds, carrying candles and singing all thirty seven verses of the Walsingham Pilgrim Hymn. Bob called to mind a previous visit when one poor, unfortunate pilgrim saw the sleeve of his anorak set alight as he jostled in the crowd. Bob wanted to share that memory with Nancy, but decided that it would be inappropriate to do so at that particular moment in time.

Arrangements had been made for all pilgrims to gather together in the hall after Benediction where light refreshments would be served. This was not compulsory of course, but it would provide an ideal opportunity for pilgrims to meet one with another. Although the group from Rhydbrychan had already acquainted themselves with the Ystrad Valley pilgrims there were two other groups there besides, one being from the parish of St. Stephen's near Rotherham and the other was from Christchurch, Maiden Hill. A goodly number responded to the invitation however, and first through the doors were Huw and Merion.

'I don't know about you butt,' said Merion, 'but I'm ready for this. It doesn't look very light to me; look - there's pasties, sausage rolls, scotch eggs as well as sandwiches. It's a genuine Christian *bun-fight.*'

'Who do you think prepared all this then?' asked Huw.

'The Sisters,' replied Meirion.

Huw began to sing, 'Sisters, sisters, there were never such devoted sisters!...'

'Don't be so disrespectful Huw,' he said. 'They've done a fine job here.'

At that moment they were approached by a tall blonde gentleman. He took Huw's hand and shook it profusely. His grin was comparable to that of someone who had heard the best joke in living memory. 'Gus,' he said as he continued to shake Huw's hand.

'I think you must be mixing me up with somebody else,' replied Huw. 'I'm not Gus, I'm Huw, Huw Martin from the parish of St. Mary Magdalene, Rhydbrychan. And you are?'

'Gus.'

'Ah! gotcha!' replied Huw. 'And where are you from?'

'I'm with the party from St. Stephen's, though you can't call it a party really. Ninety five per cent of them have a two hundred quid heating allowance and the other five percent have meals on wheels as well.' He laughed heartily at what he had said. At this point Bryn joined them.

'You must be with the St. Stephen's party,' Bryn said to him. ' But if you'll excuse me, I really need to mingle, if you get my drift.'

'Sure do mate.' said Gus then added 'Have one for me while you're at it!'

'There must be one in every parish,' thought Bryn to himself as he walked towards the priest from Maiden Hill whose face he recognised from some where in the distant past.

Meanwhile, Lillian Shanks, Hilda Grey, Pat and Martha had met three ladies from the parish of Maiden Hill. They sat together around a table close to the buffet.

'I wanted to go back.' said Martha. 'I *knew* I should go back.'

'Back where?' asked Barbara from Maiden Hill. 'Had you left something behind?'

'To the tomb.' Martha paused. 'To the tomb. As soon as I left I wanted to go back. It was like a magnet. I've never felt like that before in all my seventy-five or is it seventy six years. I'll remember this trip for ever.'

'Likewise,' said Lillian Shanks. 'It has been so spiritually uplifting.'

'Well we only arrived today, just in time for supper in fact. The peas were cold and they'd run out of lasagne. What's more, my voice is hoarse after singing all them verses of that hymn and all that standing didn't help either.' Hitherto, Barbara had experienced no divine presence.

'I'm sure that by tomorrow you'll see things quite differently,' said Pat. 'After all, you must be very tired after your long journey.'

Lucy spent the evening with Mark Johnson who was the Sacristan and Head Server in Christchurch, Maiden Hill. 'I'm leaving home soon, so to speak,' he told her. He went on to explain that he would be going to Cambridge to read Theology.

'I'm hoping to study music,' said Lucy. 'I'd like to go to one of the London Colleges if I get the grades. On the other hand, I may take a gap year and do some voluntary work overseas. I haven't really decided yet. I'll see how this AS year has gone first.'

It was well after midnight when they exchanged addresses and mobile phone numbers as they agreed that they would keep in touch. These two young people were indeed on the same wave length and had a lot of things in common, not least of which was the love they had for their respective parishes. Lucy returned to her room, and shortly afterwards, just like her fellow pilgrims, was resting in peace as it were.

All too soon the day of departure arrived and on the Thursday morning, immediately before leaving Walsingham, the group made their last visit to The Holy House where prayers were said to Our Lady and thanks offered to God for the blessings of the Pilgrimage. The musical instruments, along with the books and the luggage had been packed away before breakfast so that the pilgrims could appreciate their final moments at the Shrine. Candles were lit and then everyone stood in silent meditation. One by one they left the Shrine and made their way to the car park. 'May I speak please, Vicar?' asked Lillian Shanks once everybody had assembled.

'Of course,' Bryn replied.

'I would like to express my gratitude for such a wonderful pilgrimage. I'm sure that I speak on behalf of all those present.'

'Yes indeed,' said Hilda Grey. 'It has been most moving.'

'I'm going back home a different person,' said Martha.

'Three cheers!' called out Charles. 'Oh... er... for the Vicar I mean Martha,' and '*Hoorays*' resounded through the car park.

The journey home seemed to go quite quickly and the mini bus pulled into St. Mary Magdalene's car park shortly after five o'clock. Bryn and Huw had returned some fifteen minutes before and had taken the vestments and the books to the vestry, and placed the keyboard on the back seat of the church ready to be collected by someone from the school the following day. They required an extra keyboard to be used in their end of term concert.

'Welcome home pilgrims,' he said as the pilgrims alighted wearily from the coach. 'Does anyone need a lift or help with luggage?' Nobody did. Lucy decided to leave her guitar in church overnight and Martha rang home for a second time to check that Fred was on his way from the farm to meet her. At that very moment he drove into the car park. 'Welcome home pilgrims,' he shouted, unwittingly echoing Bryn's words. 'Did you have one helluva time guys?'

Lillian Shanks viewed him with complete disdain. 'It was the most spiritually uplifting experience ever.' She paused. 'Good afternoon all,' she added as she turned towards the gates.

Within five minutes the pilgrimage had come to an end and Bryn and Jennie were the only ones left outside the church.

'Do you feel like returning the bus now?' asked Bryn, 'or would you prefer to leave it until tomorrow? Maybe you've done enough driving for one day.'

'I'd like to take it back now please Bryn,' she replied, 'while it's still in pristine condition. Will you follow me down to the garage?'

'I'll be right behind you. I'll just lock up.' As he turned the key in the lock he reiterated with sincerity words spoken by Lillian Shanks during the Parish Pilgrimage – 'Amen! Alleluia! We have been richly blessed.'

Chapter 7: NEW NEIGHBOURS

SMART + SONS
SOLD

'Arosfa' was a detached villa type residence that had been built towards the end of the nineteenth century. It stood in small grounds adjacent to the vicarage and had been occupied for many years by Miss Annie Wilson who was a retired solicitor. She had died in Nant-y-Mynydd Nursing Home on May 7th some years before at the age of ninety six, and was laid to rest in the churchyard of St. Mary Magdalene the following week. She had outlived all her close friends, including Abraham Bont and his sister Maisie, and had often reminisced to Bryn and Jennie about the many happy evenings she had spent with them singing around the piano. 'They were such happy days,' she had said.

The large congregation at the funeral service held at the parish church confirmed how well respected and how very much loved she had been within the community. The hundreds of mourners came from all walks of life and spanned three generations. Her only surviving relative, Bernice, had flown in from Los Angeles for the funeral and had spent the following two weeks in Rhydbrychan sorting out her aunt's possessions. The local charity shops had benefited from a variety of items, including some valuable china, and there was a scheme within the locality that provided needy families with furniture and other domestic necessities. This meant that, by the time Bernice was to return to the United States, the house had been completely emptied.

'Arosfa' was put on the market in late June and, when Jennie first noticed the For Sale sign, she recalled the warm welcome that Annie had shown when they had arrived in the parish some years previously.

'Do come in and visit me sometime,' she had said, standing on tip toe with arms aloft, as she passed a dozen welshcakes over the boundary wall. 'I hope that you will be very happy here and that you will soon settle in. The parish of St. Mary Magdalene, Rhydbrychan, must be the best in the province.'

Jennie, remembering these words as she looked at the coffin as it stood in the chancel during the Requiem Mass, whole-heartedly endorsed that remark.

The house remained empty for a few years. Maybe the fact that it was in need of some upgrading was a drawback to some potential buyers. However, it was in early March 2005 when Jennie had been in the garden attending to the refuse bin, that she had heard voices coming from over the wall. She could see that a young couple had come to view the house and recognised them immediately. It was Nathan Beynon and his fiancée Natalie who were due to get married at Pont Gwallter later in the year. His mother Megan had mentioned in the Mothers' Union meeting held in January that she had already bought her outfit for the occasion. Nathan and Natalie, however, had also been looking into the possibility of purchasing a brand new property in Ystrad Fawr, therefore, due to the fact that 'Arosfa' was in need of repair, they decided to go for the 'ideal home' for first time buyers - as the new housing development had described it in the property mail.

Jennie had noticed the estate agent showing several couples around, but it wasn't until early August, soon after the Parish Pilgrimage had taken place, that the word 'SOLD' appeared on the sign. Bryn had been told by the Executor of Annie's will, and also by Bernice Wilson herself, that the church of St. Mary Magdalene was the sole beneficiary of the house sale.

Bryn and Jennie didn't have to wait long before finding out about their new neighbours. On the following Saturday morning as they were having 'elevenses' together - a rare treat in the vicarage - they heard children's voices coming from the garden next door. The kitchen window was open to allow in some air, as the predicted temperatures of 25 centigrade were becoming ever more apparent.

'Give it here you *dumbo!*' demanded a voice that Jennie believed to belong to that of a young comprehensive school pupil.

'It's mine! *Gerroff!* Super dumbo!' was the reply.

'*Dumbo!*'

'*Butt-face!*'

'*Ratface!*'

'*Redpants!*'

'*Trimmer-knickers....*' and so the name calling carried on, becoming increasingly close to the mark until one of them bawled, '*Full-kecks!!* Give me my rugby ball *now!*'

'Go and fetch it then,' somebody bellowed and, with that, Jennie and Bryn saw the rugby ball in question fly past the kitchen window.

Bryn started to get up with the intention of going into the garden to retrieve the ball and throw it back over the boundary wall, but Jennie told him to wait until someone either knocked at the door or rang the bell and asked politely if they could have the ball. They continued to enjoy their coffee, assuming that the ball was to stay in their garden until further notice. Suddenly they saw a figure running past so Jennie hurried to the open window.

'Excuse me,' she called.

'Why, what have you done?' was the ill- mannered reply, followed by a raucous yet rhythmical '*Ha!Ha!Ha!Ha!Ha!*'

'You've come into our garden without permission,' stated Jennie directly, though not unkindly.

'So what? I had to get my ball back didn't I? That stupid brother of mine, neat Pete with the very smelly feet chucked it over deliberate like. Ah, there it is!' and he lunged over, picked up the ball, fell to the ground and shrieked, '*Try!!*'

Bryn came to the window and speaking quietly but firmly to the trespasser asked,

'If it happens again would you please come to the front door and ring the bell like everyone else.'

'Do everyone kick their balls in here then?' the boy asked.

Bryn thought that the youngster was most uncouth and chose to ignore the remark. He went on to say,

'So your brother's name is Peter, and what did you say your name was?'

'I didn't,' came the abrupt reply.

'What a most unusual name!' replied Bryn with an element of sarcasm. '*I didn't. I didn't,*' he repeated emphatically. We're very pleased to meet you …*I didn't.* This is Jennie my wife and I'm the Reverend Bryn Jenkins. I'm the vicar of the parish of St. Mary Magdalene, Rhydbrychan.'

'Bible Bashers! We got this R.E. teacher in school and she's a Bible Basher too. Do you know her?'

'Perhaps,' Bryn replied. He didn't really feel like carrying on with the conversation at this point. As the intruder was leaving the premises he informed Bryn and Jennie that his name was Paul and that he would soon be moving into 'Arosfa' along with his mother Kate, her partner Mike and the stupid Redpants.

The remainder of the coffee break was spent in complete silence. Jennie was deep in thought; these new neighbours seemed to be a far cry from the dear, courteous, gracious Annie Wilson. Shortly afterwards Bryn returned to the study to deal with some correspondence but Jennie remained at the kitchen table. She saw the rugby ball flying past the window again. She hurried to the window in time to see the youngster speed past shouting, '*Scorio!!*' She was beginning to lose patience by now and called,

'Come here please. Now what did my husband tell you only a moment ago?'

'He never told me nothing. I've never seen him in my life. What's he like? Tall, dark and handsome or an ugly duckling?'

'That's enough and no lies please. It's less than five minutes since you were here before.'

This boy couldn't possibly deny that he hadn't been there just a little while earlier. If nothing else, the curly auburn hair, perhaps described more meaningfully by the true Welsh as 'cochen' would be sure to give him away anywhere. That, together with the red Welsh rugby jersey, made him a colourful exhibit.

'I don't want to spoil your fun Paul,' said Jennie, 'but..'

'I'm not Paul,' the boy interrupted.
'You're not?' questioned Jennie. 'Then who are you?'

'*My* name is Peter.'
'You look very much the same. Which of you is the elder?' asked Jennie .

'Paul, by three minutes and twenty two seconds.'

Then the penny dropped. These boys were twins, and identical twins at that. In order to avoid any confusion in the future Jennie would have to find some means of telling them apart. Maybe their eyes were different colours; she would look more closely next time.

The new neighbours moved in on a Thursday a few weeks later. It happened to be the wettest day of the summer so far that year. Bryn had left early that morning for a service in the Cathedral but, having been informed that the family were due to take up residence that day, he had told Jennie that he would make a point of welcoming them into the parish some time during the evening. Jennie had made a Shepherd's Pie for the family, which she intended to take around as soon as the removal van had left. At around mid-day she went to look through the sitting room window to see if it had gone, but the removal men were still very much hard at work. They were carrying a heavy sofa into the house and Jennie happened to notice that the man in the front seemed to be taking all the weight. His face appeared to be rather flushed. Jennie immediately became anxious and this feeling was intensified as she watched the men almost drop the product on the garden path so that the workman to the front could catch his breath. Without a second thought Jennie hurried outside.

'Is everything alright?' she asked.

'Not too bad love,' gasped the man who had been bearing most of the weight. 'We've been at it all morning; there's so much heavy stuff and still quite a bit to go yet. It's only me and Charlie today 'cos the other two boys phoned in sick. Mind you, they were alright yesterday. Good job, too! They both had expensive tickets for that football match last night.' He paused for a moment and went on to say, 'There are two fridge freezers for a start. All I need is a cuppa, but there don't seem to be no 'lectric in the house at the moment. Mike's phoned up and they're sending someone out later today. That don't help me though.'

'I'll put the kettle on and you can all come in for some light refreshments. I'm sure that you can do with a break.'

She walked around to 'Arosfa' and invited the family to come to the vicarage in about twenty minutes time. By then she would have everything ready. In fact, she was able to provide a varied lunch as there were plenty of left-overs from the evening before. The Youth Club had been there for a party to celebrate winning the diocesan baseball championship that had been held at Pont Gwallter the week before.

She spent the following ten minutes leaping around the kitchen as if she herself was engaged in a tournament of some kind, but soon she was ready for the impromptu buffet. She even decided to include the boiled potatoes that she had prepared for their own supper that evening.

Before the suggested twenty minute wait had elapsed the doorbell rang.

'*Do come in.* The door's open,' she called from the kitchen doorway. 'Come this way,' and she directed the visitors into the kitchen.

When everybody had arrived Jennie introduced herself and explained that her husband was out on business. 'I always thought that Vicars only did a one day week, now I know for sure. He's a businessman for the rest of the week is he? You must be cashing it in one way and another. Good for you! By the way, I'm Jack.Spratt's Removals…Worldwide… and this is my assistant Charlie.'

'Pleased to meet you Charlie,' said Jennie.

'Likewise,' he answered.

To say that Charlie was a man of few words was a slight exaggeration; he was a man of just one word.

The boys' mother introduced herself as Ms. Kate Chick, but expressed how much she was looking forward to becoming a common Davies as soon as she and Mike could find time to get married.

'Now please help yourselves. There's plenty here, and, boys, if you'd like to take yours into the lounge and watch the television, feel free to do so.'

They both piled their plates and skidded off into the other room. Jennie hoped that they intended neither to '*scorio!*' or '*try!*' for the duration of their visit. The adults sat informally around the kitchen table.

'What can I get you to drink?' Jennie asked politely.

'A nice cold beer will do nicely for me please,' replied Mike.

When Jennie explained that she didn't serve alcoholic beverages so early in the day, he reluctantly settled for a cup of tea with not too much milk and just a little sugar. Everyone seemed to enjoy what appeared to be a very pleasant luncheon party. Jack was the first to leave the table, giving a resounding belch as he did so, which prompted Jennie to think that perhaps Jack of Spratt's Removals …Worldwide... must have taken on a 'move' to China.

'That was *de-licious*,' he emphasised, 'but we'd best be getting back to it. Thank you very much.'
'Likewise,' said Charlie, and they left the vicarage, slamming the front door behind them.

Kate and Mike accepted Jennie's offer of a piece of fruit to finish. She could see that they had made themselves very comfortable and were in no rush to go. She was glad that the Ladies Guild meeting scheduled for that afternoon had been postponed and that she had been able to offer some hospitality to her new neighbours, and get to know a little about them. Mike was a long distance lorry driver for a fashionable department store and he was frequently away overnight. Kate had been working for some years as a teacher's aide because it meant that her hours and holidays were the same as the twins, but she had been made redundant at the end of the last academic year due to a fall in pupil numbers.

The family had been renting a house in Derwen Fawr, but the landlord had decided to sell up because he was leaving the country to spend the autumn and the winter of his life in a luxury apartment overlooking the Pacific Ocean. Unfortunately the asking price for the Derwen Fawr property was way beyond their means, so Kate and Mike had to look for something else quickly. They had felt at home as soon as they walked into 'Arosfa' and decided at once to sort out a mortgage. Kate explained that she would have to look for some sort of job soon, but for the time being there would be plenty to do in the house. She could exercise some of her DIY skills. 'I love interior decorating,' she said, 'but I'll be leaving the major improvements to Mike. We'll probably have to get the builders in at some point.'

When Jennie told them that she was a retired teacher Kate expressed her concern regarding their sons' behaviour since starting at the comprehensive school the year before. They had always been boisterous and full of life, but they were becoming more unruly and disobedient; they used words that neither she nor Mike had taught them, and she couldn't blame their father for it because he had gone before either of them had said their first word. Sometimes, she confessed, she was at her wits end. Mike said that if he earned a fat salary the boys could go private, but that was out of the question, especially now with the mortgage payments.

Kate and Mike were still chatting when the doorbell rang. It was Jack.

'*Do come in* Jack,' said Jennie. 'Would you like more tea?'

'No thanks. Can I have a word with Mike?'

'Go ahead,' said Jennie, expecting Charlie to appear and say 'Likewise.'

'Mike, did you know that you had two fridge freezers mate? We've already put one in the kitchen. Do you want me to leave this one on the van and we'll take it to the dump for you, or what?'

'Hell.. oh heck.. *no!* That one's for the garage. I keeps my beers, breezers, wines, virtual baileys, ice cubes and other essentials in that one. There's an electric point in the garage, so would you plug it in quick mate, so that I can have a few bevvies tonight?'

'I would if I could comrade. I like a cold beer myself but there's no 'lectric. Remember?'

'I do now since you mention it. I guess I'll go down the pub instead.'

'Likewise,' said Charlie who had appeared in the doorway.

The Golden Hour arrived at three o' clock precisely, when Jack came to ask Kate and Mike to go in and check if everything was alright next door. He and Charlie were ready to leave. Kate called to the boys to turn off the television, bring their lunch plates into the kitchen and follow her next door. They had been surprisingly well behaved and Jennie was most impressed with them.

'Thank you very much,' said Peter.

And thank you for letting us watch the television. I wish we had a big screen like that.'

'Come on then lads. Well done!' said Mike; He was pleased that things had gone so well. As they were making their way through the hall Jennie remembered about the Shepherd's Pie. 'Just a moment Mike. I've made a Shepherd's Pie for you all to have for supper.'

'*Yuck!*' exclaimed Paul, 'I *hate* Shepherd's Pie. They chuck it up in the canteen in school and it tastes like….' 'Thank you Jennie.' Mike interrupted quickly, anticipating what was coming next. 'You're very kind.'

Peter turned to face Jennie and lifted his arm at approximately 120 degrees and barked '*Heil!*' Jennie simply responded with a respectful '*Hwyl*.'

It was well after six o' clock when Bryn arrived home that evening. He had decided to go and visit Hywel Mason, vicar of St. Cynfelin's, Abermawr, who was recovering at home after a spell in hospital where he had been suffering from pneumonia. At one point, a week or so before, it seemed to be touch and go, but his consultant at Ysbyty Maldwyn had discharged him two days ago and Hywel already seemed to be making remarkable progress.

'I want to be back at the altar ASAP.' he had said to Bryn.

Bryn thought to himself that few others would want to be back at work so quickly after such a severe illness. By the time Bryn had arrived home all the evidence of the lunch time binge had been cleared away and the table had been laid for supper, complete with an opened bottle of Merlot.

'Jen,' said Bryn as he came into the kitchen, 'I'm feeling very tired. I think I'd prefer to wait until tomorrow before welcoming our new neighbours into the parish, but if you really would like to meet them this evening then I will attempt to muster the energy. On the other hand, they might well want to keep themselves to themselves for a few days whilst they settle in. What do you think?'

'I think that they will be very nice neighbours, though completely different to Annie of course, but very nice all the same. I hope that the twins will be able to toe the line a bit, but apart from that I see no problem at all. Kate and Mike seem very sensible people.'

'You're speaking as if with authority and you haven't had an occasion to meet them yet,' replied Bryn.

'I beg to differ Vicar. I met them at lunchtime today when we sat here around this very table,' - and she went on to give an account of the whole proceedings, even to the point of mentioning Jack Spratt's Chinese expression of gratitude.

'You are one in a million Jennie. What you have done for 'Arosfa' reminds me of what Annie did for us on our first evening here at the vicarage. Remember when she passed the welshcakes over the wall and welcomed us into the community? Well, you've done exactly the same. I hope that they will be as happy here in Rhydbrychan as we have been. But now, let's enjoy a quiet supper together.'

When they had finished they quickly cleared away the dishes and went up to bed to watch the television.

Bryn called on his new neighbours shortly after lunch the following afternoon. Kate explained that Peter and Paul had gone to the park to play football, but she was in no doubt that he would have a chance to meet them before very long. Bryn went on to say that he had already had a brief encounter with one of the boys, but that he was looking forward to meeting them both in time. (He was delighted that they had found the local park where they could score as many goals and tries as they liked without bothering anybody.) Mike, Kate and Bryn chatted amicably for the best part of an hour.

'Jennie was right.' he thought. 'These are very nice people.' As he got up to leave he said, 'It's really good to meet you and if there's anything I can do for you, please don't hesitate to ask.'

Kate quickly spoke up. 'Will you marry us as soon as we've got things straightened out by here? It shouldn't take more than a week or so till we're sorted and Mike's already arranged some annual leave.'

Bryn sat down again. It was obvious that neither Kate nor Mike had any concept of the rules and regulations laid down in the Constitution of the Church in Wales regarding the Sacrament of Marriage. He went on to explain that he would need to meet them officially to give them some guidance and instruction, and he informed them about the need to be present in church for the reading of the banns.

'Count me out,' said Mike, with a degree of nervousness. 'There's no way I'm reading in church.'

'*You* won't have to read anything Mike. I read out the names of the couple who plan to get married. It's a necessary legal procedure, but I will explain everything clearly when you come to see me in the vicarage.' They made an appointment to see Bryn in two weeks time. As Bryn was leaving Mike told him that the last time they had been inside a church was for his grandfather's funeral, but they might 'give it a go' on the coming Sunday.

When Bryn walked out of the vestry on Sunday morning, he could see his neighbours sitting in the pew that was usually occupied by Mrs. Lillian Shanks. On this occasion, she had attended the early service, as she was expecting company for lunch. Her comfortable cushion along with the colourful thick hassock must have steered the family to use that particular row of seating. Mr. Huw Martin was in the pew behind, which had been assigned to the Vicar's Warden for more than a century.

During the service he surreptitiously helped Kate and Mike to find the places in the Eucharist book and the accompanying leaflet. Bryn noticed that each time the congregation stood Peter and Paul made some erratic movements up and down and were giggling audibly. The Psalm appointed for the day was Psalm 30 and Huw Martin couldn't help but notice the boys attempting to act out the latter line of verse 10....'they do not hesitate to spit in my face.' Bryn was almost dreading going into the pulpit to deliver his sermon and his concern was not unfounded. Just as he was about to ask God that his words be acceptable in His sight, there was a terrific bang as a heavy hymnal fell to the floor. He was certain that either Peter or Paul had thrown it deliberately. He was only two or three minutes into his sermon when he happened to notice that one of them was waving at him and expressing amusement. Bryn focused immediately on Mrs. Ida Phillips, who invariably responded to his words with a gentle smile or a nod of encouragement.

When Bryn had given the blessing at the end of the service Pat began to play Beethoven's 'Ode to Joy' from the Choral Symphony. Peter and Paul immediately pushed their way out of the pew and marched quickly up the aisle bellowing, 'left, right, left, right,' until they got to the table at the back of the church where the coffee was about to be served. They both grabbed a handful of biscuits and made off through the west door. Meanwhile May and Helen had come to introduce themselves to Kate and Mike, and to welcome them to the parish.

'Are you able to join us for coffee this morning?' asked Helen.

'Thank you, but I think we'd better get back to the boxes,' replied Mike. 'We've still got a lot of unpacking left to do.'

'It's very nice to see a young family amongst us,' said Margaret Jones. 'I hope that you will be very happy here at St. Mary Magdalene's. We're a very friendly crowd you know.'

Mike didn't have the heart to tell her that they had only 'given it a go' as it were, and he for one, at this point, felt loath to make a habit of it.

'It's like this, see,' he said to Bryn when they met him regarding the wedding plans. 'I got confused with all that standing up and sitting down and I couldn't keep up with you when you were bowing your head all the time. Talk about a pain in the neck! And the way those two lads behaved, well, that gave me a pain somewhere else I can tell you. I felt ashamed.'

Bryn assured him that the children weren't the first, and neither would they be the last, to act up during a service; boys would be boys! Maybe they would like to try the Sunday School instead. Mike and Kate took some comfort from this observation. Mike said that they would take a crack at another service sometime soon.

The wedding was decided for the first Saturday in November. Mike had checked his roster and had discovered that he was off until the Sunday of the following week so along with his pre-arranged leave he would have almost two weeks off work. This also coincided with the children's half term. This meant that the children could go and spend a few days with Kate's parents who had moved to Burnham-on-Sea. They always loved going there and this would leave Kate and Mike with some time for themselves. They were thinking that they might take a short break to Bruges.

The couple attended church on each Sunday that their banns were read and also on the two Sundays before the wedding. They were beginning to feel more comfortable in what had initially been a somewhat unfamiliar situation. Peter and Paul had started attending Sunday School. They had taken to Uncle James the moment they had met him in swimming club and it was *his* words and actions, rather than those of Jesus, which were the attraction at present. They behaved impeccably during their Sunday School classes and even raised their hand to offer answers to questions in order to impress. On one occasion Uncle James had asked the class what they thought God looked like.

'He's got a long grey beard,' said Sheree with confidence.

'I don't think he wears glasses,' said Will, 'because he can see everything.'

Hywel was the next to speak. 'Well... he's got *very, very,* big hands, because he can hold the whole world in them.'

'All these are good ideas,' stated Uncle James. 'Would anyone else like to say something?'

Paul put up his hand. 'Yes Paul?' asked Uncle Jim with a smile of encouragement.

Paul put his head to one side as if in deep thought. '*I* think,' he said slowly, 'that he looks like *you*.'

Immediately the class was in uproar, with some of the children literally falling off their seats laughing. 'Imagine God in a pair of speedos!' laughed Will.

'Well...he *is* Mr. Universe,' observed Andy.

'Enough!' shouted Uncle James authoritatively. The children immediately settled down. There was complete silence and when he confirmed that Paul was absolutely 'spot on' the class was completely stunned.

'Well done Paul. *Very* well done. Would you like to explain to us why you said that?'

'I didn't mean that he only looked like you. I meant that he looked like a person, because Jesus says in the Bible something like, '*if you have seen me you have seen my father*', so I thought that God must look like an ordinary human being. That's what I meant really.'

'I couldn't have wished for a better answer. Now then, let's all draw a picture of God and perhaps we can put them on display in the Children's Corner at the back of the church.'

Kate and Mike arranged a very quiet wedding. Only very close family had been invited, along with their neighbours, Bryn and Jennie. May and Helen prepared a magnificent floral pedestal of red and white roses that was placed to the left of the altar and they had also been responsible for the bridal bouquet that complimented the arrangement, and the red and white buttonholes for male and female guests respectively.

The weather on the Wedding Day turned out to be warm and sunny. Mike took his place, front right of the church well before the scheduled mid-day start, together with his brother Anthony who was to be his best man. Since this wedding was less formal than most, Kate's mother Selina and Mike's parents Ronald and Ann, came in the same taxi, along with Peter and Paul. The twins were immaculately dressed in dark grey suits, cream shirts and pink ties. They had willingly forsaken their worn-out trainers for a pair of black patent lace-ups, on the condition that they could be returned to the shop the following day. Kate's sister Judy and brother-in-law Jo had shared a taxi with Ray and Ruth, Mike's brother and sister.

The only absent friend was Jeanne from California. She had been Kate's best friend in childhood but had taken up a teaching post in Pasadena the year after she qualified. She had in her 'reply with regret' invited the bride and groom to holiday at her home at any time. The boys could enjoy her large swimming pool whilst Kate and Mike 'got on with what ever they wanted to be getting on with' at the time. Apart from Jeanne then, everybody was present and correct.

At mid-day precisely the bride appeared at the church of St. Mary Magdalene. She looked beautiful in her cream ankle length dress and her shoes were of a corresponding colour. May and Helen had made her a magnificent headdress of red and white roses and she looked fantastic from head to toe. Bryn met her at the west door and gave some reassurances before she walked into the church, holding onto her father Horace's arm somewhat nervously. As she walked down the aisle to Pat's rendering of Lohengrin's Bridal March, she was amazed to see that so many of the pews were occupied. Her eyes were soon to meet those of Uncle James, who blew her a kiss. This was followed almost immediately by a wink accompanied by a suggestive gesture from Charles Harris and, as she was passing the pew where a Mrs. Lillian Shanks always sat, she heard her whisper, 'God bless you dear. All the very best.'

She felt quite overwhelmed by the strength of support that the people of this community were giving them. The service was beautiful and Bryn's address was outstanding. He explained that, in a sense, the couple would never be the same again. Although they would look the same, enjoy the same music as they had until now and participate in activities that they derived pleasure from, everything would be different because the couple were now to become one in the sight of God. There would be hard times ahead as well as the good times; life was not all sweetness and light, but there was always that third person to help and sustain them.

God would always be there with them and for them until their lives' end. When they went into the vestry to sign the registers Lucy came forward with a few children from her Sunday School class to sing a mantra that she had composed specially for the occasion. It was called 'Your Wedding Day' and expressed how two would be made one and the presence of the Holy Spirit would be with them throughout their lives.

The congregation was so inspired that they spontaneously applauded the contribution. Soon after Mr. & Mrs. Michael Davies processed down the aisle as husband and wife to Pat's rendition of Beethoven's 'Ode to Joy'. Peter and Paul respectfully remained standing in the pew and, to Mike's surprise, they both said in unison, 'Congratulations Mum and Dad.'

A great deal of excitement followed the service as well wishers spoke to the newly-weds. Kate insisted that they should have a photograph with everybody who had been present at the ceremony. They had to wait for Pat, however. She was obviously sorting out her music for the Eucharist the following day. Meanwhile, young Gemma and Sally presented the Bride and Groom with a specially designed love spoon as a gift from the parish. Lillian Shanks managed to surreptitiously slip an envelope with a £50 cheque enclosed into the Groom's jacket pocket. It was only afterwards that she thought that the suit might be hired.

The Bridal Party then began to walk to 'Yr Hen Efail' for the wedding reception. They left the church grounds to rapturous applause and cheers, and were showered with the confetti that had been banned until they had left the churchyard. Their idea of a quiet wedding had turned out to be anything but! However, they were both having a wonderful day. The three course meal was delicious and the speeches that followed were short but amusing. Ray reminded Mike of the time when they used to telephone people they found spontaneously by name in the directory, like a Mr. Fish and they would ask him if he was frying that night and did he do green peas as well, or a Mr. Shepherd and did *'Baa! Baa! Black Sheep have any wool?'* Now, with the 1471 call-back connection, such capers were impossible. Gone were some of the good old days of childish pranks perhaps, Mike was willing to admit, but he and Kate had a lifetime of good days to look forward to and to share.

As time went by they became active members of the parish of St. Mary Magdalene and it was an emotional moment for the whole congregation when, the following year in the month of May and on the day of Pentecost, the whole family knelt together on the chancel steps to be confirmed by Bishop Anselm. Farthest away from the family's thoughts at that moment was the comment that Peter had made the night before….'If he's 'andsome then Quasimodo must have been absolutely stunning!'

After confirmation the twins were included on the acolytes' rota and they thoroughly enjoyed participating in this way. Not once did they attempt to blow out the candles or fool around in the processions; perhaps this was because Father Jeffrey, who was ultimately responsible for organising the rotas, ensured that they never actually teamed up together for a service. Although they were becoming much more responsible and mature he couldn't rule out a possible cackle or smirk as the Gospel was read from the nave, and this would be most inappropriate. Consequently, Paul always carried out his duties with Hywel and Peter teamed up with Will.

In time the boys graduated to become servers and they always performed their duties with reverence and respect. In fact, Bryn thought that they must be the most devout servers in the Diocese and, when they participated in the service to commemorate Bryn's twenty fifth anniversary of priesthood, he sensed a certain sanctity that he couldn't really explain.

'There's something about those boys that I can't put my finger on,' he had said to Jennie when they arrived home that night. 'They are both so very devout.'

Bryn became increasingly impressed with their exceptional manners and their readiness to help out in any way, not only in church worship, but around and about in the community at large. They were often seen going shopping for some of the residents of Waun Wen, or helping them out with some DIY. When the A level examination results came out both Peter and Paul discovered that they had done extremely well. The two of them achieved an A* in Religious Studies and A in Music. Peter had a B grade in History and Paul achieved a B in English. Peter had been accepted at Leeds University to read History and Paul had been offered a place at the University of Wales, Bangor to study Music. Neither of them wanted to take a gap year; they were both keen to continue with their higher education.

Their parents were overjoyed at the boys' examination results and, later that week they threw a party at 'Arosfa' to celebrate their success. Many of the congregation of St. Mary Magdalene were present including Uncle James,

Lillian Shanks, May and Helen, Charles Harris, Pat Lewis, Jan Bevan and others.

'You two boys are a credit to your parents and to the parish,' said Lillian Shanks as she handed them each a congratulations card with a voucher to the value of £20 enclosed.

Charles Harris also congratulated the pair, but made a bee-line for Kate and gave her a sloppy kiss along with a loud 'Bravo' to the proud mum. He just couldn't resist the opportunity of an encounter however brief. Mike gave a moving speech followed by a toast to the young men's continued success.

Some years later, shortly before Bryn's retirement, they telephoned him to ask if he would be willing to give each of them a reference; they had both felt a calling to the priesthood, so they were offering themselves for ordination.

'I will be delighted to do so,' Bryn had replied. Both Peter and Paul did their training at St. Dyfrig's Theological College in Heddfan. By then there was no fear of the principal or the tutors getting them mixed up, since whilst Peter was in university, he had dyed his hair brown and Paul had recently become blonde. Three years later in St. Deiniol's Cathedral an elderly Bishop Anselm ordained Peter and Paul as deacons in the Church in Wales, and Bryn felt privileged to participate in the laying on of hands which is such a significant part of the service. As he returned to his seat he had a quick flashback to when he first made their acquaintance. He smiled to himself at the memory, then, kneeling in prayer, he thanked God for these two new members of the clergy and asked His blessing on their respective ministries.

Before giving the final blessing, Bishop Anselm requested that the congregation be seated.

'This is a very special day in the lives of those who have been ordained as priests and deacons here today, and as a congregation we wish you Godspeed in the years ahead. During my time as Bishop of St. Deiniol's I have had the honour and privilege of ordaining 116 men and women as ministers in the church. This, however, has been my last Ordination service, for, as you probably know, I shall be retiring early next year. Nevertheless, we can see quite clearly that where one door closes another one opens; where one chapter in life ends another one begins. God is forever working out his purpose and His Almighty plan. So then,

Rejoice in the Lord always

And again I say, Rejoice!

Let us give thanks to the Lord our God

For it is meet and right so to do.

He paused momentarily then said, 'Let us pray.' The congregation knelt or sat for the blessing that followed. 'May the blessing of God Almighty, the Father, the Son and the Holy Spirit be with you and with all those whom you treasure in your hearts this day and every day. Amen.'

The congregation at the crowded cathedral responded with an ardent and assured '***Amen***.' Alpha and Omega had, that day, fulfilled another part of his omnipotent and omniscient plan.

About the Author

Evelyn Evans was brought up in Bargoed in the Rhymney Valley. She attended the Parish of St Gwladys, where she graduated from Sunday School pupil to Sunday School teacher and later to Sunday School Superintendent. A member of the Church choir, assistant organist and member of the PCC and the Drama Group, she played a full part in Parish life. Eventually she married the young curate, and they have been happily married for 35 years.

Evelyn has worked as a teacher of pupils with special educational needs. Every day brought challenges and uncertainties, and also wonderful memories. As a clergy wife she has shared people's joys and sorrows, provided millions of cups of tea and coffee, hundreds of litres of soup and dozens of casserole dishes in addition to a handful of Sonrise Breakfasts on Easter morning.

Evelyn looks back on these years with fondness and gratitude.

Lightning Source UK Ltd.
Milton Keynes UK
03 March 2011

168634UK00001B/5/P